The Diary of a Side Chick 3

A Naptown Hood Drama

Tamicka Higg'

© 2015

Disclaime.

This book contains sexually explicit content that is intended for ADULTS ONLY (+18)

2

Chapter 1

Desirae had really been stuck in her feelings for a few days after she and Shawna had gotten out of lockup downtown. She could not lie to herself anymore, as she had tried to do. It was nice the way she and Shawna teamed up and surprised Tron. The fact that he just so happened to be getting out of the shower when the two of them showed up in that townhouse was only the icing on the cake. After they dragged his ass downstairs and into the living room, they jumped on him again – letting out their frustration until they were exhausted and just ready to be through with it.

Even now, a few days later, she couldn't believe who Tron was truly turning out to be. Sure, she knew that she was fucking around with an unfaithful man, considering that the terms of their relationship had always been him "stopping by" when he had time after the restaurant. Desirae shook her head just on that thought alone, as she sat in her living room, lying sideways on her couch. The sunlight beamed into her living room from the bright snowy day outside. "Restaurant," she said, as she shook her head. It almost made her sick to her stomach to think about how even that had been a lie, and she never picked up on it.

"I wonder if that nigga's name is even Tron," she began to ask herself. After awhile, though, she figured that much about him had to be true. After all, if his name really wasn't Tron, then his chick Shawna wouldn't have called him that. There was just so much she didn't know about him. And while she may not be showing with his baby just yet, she knew that it would only be a matter of time. She patted her stomach, hating for one minute that she had ever given an ounce of thought to having an abortion.

Desirae realized just how smart of a chick she was. While she hated that she got into a fight over a man, and wound up spending a night in the Marion County jail downtown over the situation, she had figured out why Tron kept bringing up the idea of abortion so much. She knew now that he tried to plant the idea in her head and let her know that it might be the better idea.

"Fuck that nigga," she said, thinking of the way Tron played mind games with her. Desirae had figured out that Tron was trying to get her to get rid of the baby so that he could get back with

3

Shawna. In the confines of her own place, and after the fact, Desirae could allow herself to stand in Shawna's shoes for a moment. She imagined dedicating herself to and living with a dude, only to find out that he was over on the other side of the city fucking someone else and doing everything in his power to cover it up. At the same time, though, Desirae figured that if she were in Shawna's shoes, things would be at least a little bit different. The difference with Tron cheating on that Shawna chick was that he was doing it with something better on the other side of town. Desirae looked down at her body – a body that practically turned heads, especially when she walked down the street in the hood. A nigga would be hard-pressed to find a chick that had more going on that she did to be fucking around with. Desirae cracked a smile, feeling grateful that she was blessed when it came to physical beauty because everyone else is not always so lucky.

"Damn, where is she at?" Desirae asked herself, taking a break from her thoughts. Her girl Reese was supposed to be headed over. It was now going on five o'clock in the afternoon and Reese was supposed to be free around three.

Desirae hadn't seen her girl since before everything happened at Clarke's. She was trying to fill her in on it all the day she and Shawna left Tron at the townhouse, but Reese had been busy. Something or another had come up with her family, and Desirae respected that. Being the real woman that she was, Desirae made it a point to not think just about herself when it came to their friendship. With all of this snow outside, though – a good three more inches had fallen on Indianapolis just last night alone – Desirae was starting to get a little worried. She didn't want to come across as being invasive or anything, but she wanted to make sure that everything was all right. On top of that, she knew that Reese was probably dying to hear what had happened.

Desirae grabbed her phone from between two couch cushions and called Reese. She found herself getting a little more worried when the phone continued ringing, not stopping until Reese picked up on the fourth ring.

"Hello?" Reese said.

"Girl, you alright?" Desirae asked. "You said you was gon be headed over here when you got off work and shit, but you ain't came yet. I was getting kind of worried with this snow and shit, girl."

4

"Girl, you won't believe this mess," Reese said.

"What?" Desirae asked, clearly interested. "What mess? What you talkin' bout?"

"Well, okay," Reese said, starting to explain. "I got off work later. You know, I was supposed to get off at three but, because of the snow making a couple of my coworkers late, or so they say, I didn't wind up walking out of there until almost four fifteen."

Desirae thought about it for a minute – how that was forty five minutes ago. Reese was only coming from downtown. Even in semi-deep snow, the main streets coming out of downtown were always pretty clear. School had been closed, so there wasn't a ton of school busses and teachers and whatnot out on the roads for that afternoon, either.

"Yeah," Desirae said.

"So, anyway," Reese said. "I get on Madison and head out south, you know coming by the Lilly Center, and this car lost control just as we was crossing under the highway."

"Girl, you kidding," Desirae said, now hearing how shook up Reese was from it all in her voice as she explained. "Did he get close to you?"

"It was some white lady," Reese said. "And yeah, I mean I thought she was about to push me through the bridge barricade and down onto whatever-that-street-is below…Morris, I think. Girl, my life flashed before my eyes. I pulled over though and called the police and stuff for the lady. Now they here."

"Girl, if you not up for coming over and shit, I completely understand," Desirae said. "I mean, girl, that is some scary shit. You ain't gotta risk your life and all to come out here."

"Desirae, girl, it's okay," Reese said. "I'm fine and already talked to the police and stuff about what I saw. They getting ready to carry the woman to the hospital and tow her car. You know this is a big, busy road."

"Yeah, it is," Desirae said, nodding.

"I'mma be there in like fifteen minutes," Reese said. "Girl, I gotta hear what done happened now. You know how life is. It is always something."

Desirae smirked for a second, thinking about how just a few night ago, she was carried out of work in handcuffs and downtown in the back of an Indianapolis Metropolitan Police car. In the backseat of that thing, she felt like an animal. It was a feeling that she never wanted to feel again. And if she ever were to go through it again, it would not be over some nigga who wouldn't even acknowledge her.

"Ain't that the truth," Desirae said. "Alright, girl. I'll see you when you get here. The door already open and I'm ready to spill it cause you not gon' believe this shit."

"Okay, okay," Reese said. "Be there in a minute, girl. Bye."

"Bye."

Desirae hung up then dropped her phone into her lap. Now she was coming to another crossroads in her life. The following day after going to jail for getting into it with Tron's chick, when she and the chick left from beating Tron's ass over at his place, she called her manager at work. As much as Desirae knew deep down that she was far better than working at some department store, she couldn't lie to herself that the store paid all right and gave her enough hours that she could live on. On top of that, she was a smart enough woman to know that when you've got a baby on the way, some money is better than no money.

At the same time, she was nervous when calling about her job because she knew just how much of a bitch the human resources lady would be. The human resources manager for the mall store location, Kim, was always so jealous of Desirae and the attention she got from the male customers. The fact of the matter is that no matter what kind of outfit Desirae wore to work, her shape was just too much to hide. With Kim being tall and thin and rather flat chested, Desirae could pick up right away that she wished she was getting some of that same attention. Desirae's relationship, for lack of a better word, with Kim only got worse during the holiday season. Desirae remembered clearly how some man had been showing Kim a little bit of attention out on the floor. When Desirae was sent by her supervisor to go do something, she had no choice but to walk by Kim and the guy talking. And of course, at no fault of Desirae's other than being purely blessed, the man's eyes slipped away from Kim and followed her down the aisle. Ever since then, Kim had been acting shitty toward Desirae.

Desirae discovered that day that Kim was still salty about her stealing the attention a couple of months ago. Effective immediately, she was terminated. Furthermore, Kim went on to tell Desirae that

6

she might have considered giving her another chance at keeping her position with Clarke's since she was indeed provoked and attacked if only she had not dressed so provocatively when she came to work. Without even thinking, Desirae, who now knew that she really didn't have anything to lose, just went ahead and let Kim have a little piece of her mind.

"Bitch!" Desirae said into her phone, still sitting out in her car just having returned from Tron's place. "Provocative? Are you serious? You just mad… I don't even believe this mess. I was always professional with what I wore and you gon' call it provocative. Shit, I wore better outfits and stuff than you did."

Kim told Desirae, in a very condescending manner that let Desirae know that she was on the other end getting at least a little bit of pleasure out of terminating her, that she wasn't wearing the right kind of clothes for her body type. Desirae just shook her head and started laughing.

"You too much," she had said. "And you just mad that you ain't get this kind of body like me. That's all this is. I don't even fuckin' need that job. Fuck y'all."

As Desirae lay across her couch, thinking about all of that and what that meant as she was now in the early stages of pregnancy and had no job. One minute she would shake her head and almost laugh at how the world always seemed to fall on her head at the worst times. But the urge to laugh faded as she thought about the severity of her situation. It wasn't like she saved money the way she ought to. She had enough in her bank account to last her a good couple of months, but she knew that she was going to need some income. *Shit*, she thought, *I wasn't born rich or nothing.*

Within no time, Reese was knocking at the door.

"Girl, I told you it was open," Desirae announced.

The door swung open and Reese came walking in. "Damn, it's windy as fuck out there," she said as she pushed the door closed and began taking her coat off. "I'm here."

"Good," Desirae said. "Hurry up and take your coat off so I can get started with my story. You are not gon' believe this shit one bit when I tell you," Desirae added, slapping her palms together. "I mean, for real, Reese. This shit is unreal that I just don't know how to fuckin' feel."

"Okay, okay," Reese said, smiling. "Let me get this coat off and get myself something to eat and we can talk."

"Something to eat?" Desirae asked. "Girl, I ain't got no food in here."

"Desirae, girl," Reese said. "You always say that. You be having food. You just don't wanna share. Stop being like that."

Desirae smirked and rolled her eyes. "Niggas," she said, shaking her head.

"That's right," Reese said. "And I'm the guest. Look, girl, just go ahead and start telling me the story and shit while I'm getting me something to eat and drink."

"And you want something to drink?" Desirae said. "Aw hell naw."

Reese looked at Desirae as she was walking into the kitchen, squinting her eyes her direction until she disappeared. "Girl, whatever," she said from the kitchen. "So, what happened? You know I wanna know."

"Okay," Desirae said. "So where do I start?"

"Damn, is it like that?" Reese asked, pouring herself some Kool-Aid.

"Girl, yes," Desirae said and smacked her palms together. "I guess I'mma start with when I was up at Clarke's. Okay, so I was at work, you know, doin' my thing, lookin' good for any of them niggas who come walkin' through there."

"Of course," Reese said.

"And guess who come up in the store and make a bee-line, straight for my fuckin' counter like she was on a mission or some shit," Desirae said.

"Who?" Reese asked, wanting to know. "Girl, who?"

"Tron's chick, Shawna," Desirae answered.

Just then, Desirae could hear the refrigerator door close and saw Reese's head peek out from behind the wall. Her eyes looked as if they were about to pop out of her head she was so fascinated by what she had just heard.

"Are you serious?" Reese asked.

Desirae nodded her head. "Girl, yes," she said. "I guess she remembered me from the day her and the other chick had come into the store. When she saw me up at the club that Saturday night, looking ten times better than her and waiting on Tron to come out just like she was, she must have connected the dots."

Reese went back into the kitchen and went on with getting her little snack together. "Okay, go on, go on," she insisted.

"So, yeah," Desirae said. "She comes up in there and comes right for me and, you know it, some shit gets started. I mean, she just came in there talking all sorts of disrespectful. And you know me…you know I don't put up with no disrespect from nobody, I don't care who you is. Certain things I just am not gon stand for cause I ain't that chick. I guess ain't nobody tell her that, but anyway."

Just then, Reese came from around the corner with a ham sandwich and her glass of grape Kool-Aid. She sat down at the opposite end of the couch from Desirae, causing Desirae to have to move her feet out of the way.

"Well, damn," Desirae said. "Excuse me for being in your way."

"Girl, stop doing the most," Reese said, munching on her sandwich and washing it down with her drink. "Go on with the story."

"So, yeah," Desirae said. "Like I was saying, she come up in to my fuckin' job and is talkin' all sorts of reckless to me cause she knows I gotta stay professional with my shit because I'm at work and all and I'm a classy chick. And like I said, next thing you know we goin' back and forth and shit cause she just went too far. Before I know it, this bitch done put her hands on me."

"Girl, you is lyin'," Reese said, shaking her head as she drank from her cup. "All this happen up in Clarke's, up at the mall. She really came up to your job and started some shit with you?"

"Girl, yes," Desirae answered, nodding her head. She slapped her palms together again.

"So, how did that go?" Reese asked.

Desirae looked at Reese, with this look on her face that told Reese that she should have known better than to ask her a question like that. "Girl," Desirae said. "You know how that went…you know I took it there with her. I was at work, so I went a little nice on her. She prolly don't know that, but it's whatever. I really didn't want to take it there with her. But the story get crazier than that, Reese. The shit gets crazier than that."

9

"Girl, what?" Reese asked. "How can it get crazier than her coming up to your job to get a beat down? I mean…"

"I'm getting there," Desirae said. "I'm getting there. So the police come, of course. Good for her cause they pulled me off her ass when I was really gettin' in my feelings over what she had made me do. And they arrest us, putting the handcuffs on us and shit."

Reese clearly looked shocked. She had been so busy with helping her family move in the dead of winter that she felt so out of the loop when she went for even just a few days without talking to Desirae. Desirae was her girl and was always the one of the two of them that really lived life and took whatever came her way. In so many ways, Reese saw Desirae as being so strong. At the same time, Reese couldn't believe what kind of situation she had suddenly found herself in…and all over that Tron. Looking at her girl Desirae explain everything, it made Reese really start to wonder just how good Tron's dick must be for this to be happening.

"Are you serious?" Reese asked.

Desirae nodded. "Hell yeah, girl," she answered. "I got arrested and spent the night with her ass down in Marion County."

"Downtown on Washington?" Reese asked for clarification.

"Girl, yes," Desirae said. "But anyway, once we got out we was all chilled out and shit. I mean, I felt so damn stupid behind them bars. Just knowing that we got into it like that, in public, over some dude is enough for me. I was lucky that they decided to not press charges because they couldn't get a straight enough story, I guess, to figure out who to charge. Plus, with all these murders and home invasions they got going in Nap right now, they betta be worrying about the big shit in all reality."

"Girl, you right about that," Reese said. "So what happened after y'all got out?"

"I mean," Desirae started, shrugging and rolling her eyes. "We made up and shit, you know. Took the high road and all that. The crazy part is that we got to talking and guess what I find out when I was talking to her?"

"Girl, what?" Reese asked.

"Well, you remember how Tron was talking to me about going and having an abortion? Well, I know now why he kept bringing it up like that, like every other sentence. Apparently Tron was trying to make up and get back with her. The two of them had met up and even talked."

Reese wondered about the other chick's point of view as her own girl Desirae told her the story about what all had happened. She listened closely the entire time. However, in the back of her mind, she was wondering what in the world would possess Tron's chick to want to go back to him. What in the world could be so good that the dude could have a side chick for months that you find out about and you still decid to even entertain the idea of going back? Reese was really starting to wonder. She just could not help it at this point.

"Girl, that is ridiculous," Reese said, quickly, as she noticed Desirae was waiting on her response.

"Girl, what was you thinkin' bout?" Desirae asked. "You was lookin' lost there for a second."

"I was just thinking," Reese started, trying to quickly come up with the right thing to say. "I mean, I was just thinking about how some dudes are just so dirty with the shit they do. I'm sittin' here listening to you and all and it just amazes me how they do real chicks so dirty."

Desirae smiled, nodding her head. At that moment, she could really see that her and Reese had been meant to be friends. Reese was always one hundred with what she thought and she had logic. As Desirae got older, she learned just how hard that was to find in another chick. She suddenly felt even better about telling Reese about what all was happening with Tron. She felt good getting it off of her chest, and was happy that she was doing so with someone she could really trust.

"Exactly," Desirae said, slapping her palms together. "I mean these dudes don't be knowing what they have in chicks like me and you. It just don't make no sense. But anyway, girl, let me finish the story so you'll really understand. Once we got to talking and stuff, the next day when we got released and shit, on the street downtown, we wound getting a ride back to Clarke's and riding over to Tron's place."

"No!" Reese said, now needed to set her glass down on the coffee table. She remembered that for months Desirae would talk from time to time about Tron only fucking her over at her place. She never even knew or had heard of where he lived. "Girl, was it nice?"

Desirae nodded. "Yeah," she answered. "I mean, it is a townhome and shit. Two floors. Don't remember looking for how many bedrooms. The…place…is…laid…out."

Reese wondered how that made Desirae feel – to see what kind of life Tron was giving to the other chick.

"So," Desirae continued. "We went on upstairs, as his boy Tyrese was leavingt, who I met up at the club that Saturday night, remember? Yeah, so me and her head upstairs and we just so happen to find Tron getting out of the shower."

Reese, who just grabbed her cup to take a sip, choked. Instantly, she imagined Tron, filling in the gaps based on the few seconds that she'd seen him walk from the door of Desirae's apartment to get into his car. It was the only time that Reese had ever seen him. However, she remembered his swag; his tall, lean-looking body.

"He was getting out of the shower?" Reese asked. "Girl, you for real?"

Desirae nodded. "Hell yeah," she answered. "And you shoulda seen his face when he saw the two of us standing there. I kid you not, it looked like he had just seen a ghost or two. Like I don't even remember his ass blinking."

"I guess he wouldn't be," Reese said, snickering. "That was the last thing he ever expected to see."

"Hold up, girl," Desirae said. "But there is more. There is more. So me and chick cool down, head over there, and find him getting out of the shower upstairs. He lookin' like his life has just come to an end…nigga was lookin' like he was staring dead into a couple of headlights on a dark road. Before I know it, me and chick done said our words to the nigga, who of course is cowering like he some little boy."

"Of course," Reese said, rolling her eyes.

"Right," Desirae said. "Exactly what I was thinking. And once again, he do me wrong like he always do. He talk to her first, but she ain't even on that shit no more. I can see it all over her face. That chick, Shawna, is really through with his ass. Hell, I was getting my licks in and shit when we jumped on his ass, but she was really goin' hard. I was like damn."

"Y'all jumped on him?" Reese asked, knowing that she wouldn't believe this if it wasn't Desirae telling her."

Desirae smacked her lips together and nodded. "Girl, yes," she answered. "And when I tell you we was givin' that nigga the business..."

"Y'all went that hard?" Reese asked, smiling.

"Girl, yes," Desirae said. "We was beatin' that niggas ass like we was a couple of niggas our damn selves. He kept ducking and shit out of the way, but we would just stay on his ass. Before we know it, he done made his way out into the upstairs hallway and shit and going down the stairs."

"Damn," Reese said.

"Right," Desirae said. "I mean, sometimes you just don't know your own strength. Hell, I started to get in my feelings and shit when we was at it. I mean, I really got to thinking about how I was pregnant with his baby and he kept insinuating, on the phone and shit, that he would support me if I decided to get rid of the baby. I mean, I could really tell that he was starting to push that shit because he brought it up, I never did."

"Right," Reese said. "Exactly. He brought that shit up."

"The nigga really should be happy that he gon' have me as the mother of his child if you want to know the truth," Desirae said. "A lot of niggas can't say they got a child by a chick as bad as me. And that is just a fact, and it's like he don't wanna acknowledge that. But girl, I swear to God I am so through and over this shit."

"You not gon' fuck around with him no more, girl?" Reese asked.

"Why should I?" Desirae asked, clearly looking as if she thought Reese's question was a dumb question. "I mean, really? You tell me?"

"Shit, I ain't know," Reese said. "It's probably better that you just be done with his ass anyway. I mean, you done really put yourself out on a limb for him and he just don't sound, to me, like he trying to reach back and get what he know he want. I mean, if he ain't happy with his chick, then why don't he just end it?"

"Girl, exactly," Desirae said. "That is the same shit I be wondering about. He said that everything about me is better than her, and I don't be on no shit when he come over here. He come over here and get to relax without all the extra shit that she bring. And I could tell from talkin' to her that she probably ain't got what it take to keep a man like Tron."

13

"Why you say that?" Reese asked, without even thinking.

Desirae looked at Reese and smiled. "Girl, that dick," she said.

"It's that good?" Reese asked, truly interested in what Desirae was talking about now.

Desirae looked up at the ceiling, thinking of the perfect way to describe it as she slapped her palms together for the umpteenth time. "Now, I will give him that," she said. "I ain't never had no shit like that. Deep, but not too deep. Thick, but not too fat. And how it be so hard."

Reese's face lit up with excitement, hearing Desirae describe Tron's manhood. In every way, it sounded so good to her.

"But that shit ain't drive me as crazy as it drove his chick, that Shawna," Desirae said. "I mean, she really losing herself over it and I am so glad I ain't dip down that low like she done did. I mean, coming up to somebody job and starting a fight over some dude? That is just low."

"Yeah, that is," Reese said, still trying to imagine what Tron was bringing to the bedroom that would make his chick and Desirae act like that. "I guess it make y'all act that way."

"Girl, not me," Desirae said. "Not no more. I don't even wanna be bothered with his ass, but I already know that I'mma have to be now."

"I mean, yeah," Reese said. "You are having his baby and shit."

"Right," Desirae starting to get a serious look on her face. "That is actually part of the problem now that you mention it."

"What you mean?" Reese asked.

"Well, I called up to my job when I got out and shit," Desirae explained. "No matter what, I was gon' explain to them that I was attacked. But that bitch Kim is who I had to deal with."

"Ain't she the chick in hiring or something that be hatin' on you?" Reese asked, for clarification.

"Exactly, that's her ass," Desirae answered. "And I could tell when I was talkin' to her that she still can't get over the fact that I look ten times better than her. Long story short, though, she told me that I was terminated and would get my last check in a couple weeks or some shit."

14

Reese got a really serious look on her face, as she'd heard her girl, who she knew was having the child that would probably be her Godchild, say something that she truly wished was not the case. Last thing in the world she needed was to be pregnant and looking for a job. Reese had a few cousins, on both her mother's and father's sides of the family, who had either been fired or laid off when they were pregnant. It was like employers did not even want to touch them, for the simple fact that pregnant chicks would be off work for an extended amount of time within months of being hired.

"She came up to your job and attacked you and they fired you?" Reese asked.

Desirae, not liking the overall summary of the situation, nodded in agreement. "Basically, girl," Desirae said. "Basically. That is the shit that happened to me girl. I told you that you wasn't gon' believe that shit."

"Desirae, what are you gonna do?" Reese asked. "I mean, I ain't try'na be up in your bank account or nothing, but do you think you gon' be able to hold over like that?"

There was a long pause of silence where Desirae just did not know what to say. Well, she knew that the word *no* wanted to slip out of her lips. For whatever reason, though, she just knew that she would have to do something. More importantly, she knew how much Reese looked up to her in a way. She had to keep up her front of being strong.

"I'll be alright," Desirae said. "Don't you worry, Reese. I'll be alright."

"Desirae," Reese said, in a very serious tone. "That's not what I asked you. I didn't ask you if you would be alright. I mean, this shit is serious girl. I don't know if you know that or not. You ain't even been to the doctor yet about being pregnant, have you?"

Desirae shook her head. "No," she answered. "I mean, now how I'mma go. Ain't like I got health insurance."

Reese's mouth hung open. "Okay, but," she said, hesitantly, "you can find services and stuff that help pregnant, unwed mothers."

"Well, I thought about asking my mama if she would put me back on her health insurance and shit, since I ain't twenty-four or twenty-five or whatever the cut-off age is."

15

Reese had not even thought about Desirae's family. That was a totally different dynamic to this situation that would have some fireworks too, to say the least.

"That's right, girl," Reese said. "You ain't even told your mother yet, have you?"

There was a long pause where Desirae was thinking about her mother and what she would say. She couldn't lie to herself. That thought had come up several times over the last so-many days. Whenever she would think about what her mother would say, she automatically started to wonder about the church. Desirae didn't see her family as being overly religious. However, church was indeed the place they all met up at least once a week and talked – the place where they meet and Desirae is not there.

Desirae shook her head. "Girl, naw," she answered. "I ain't told her yet. I'm going to when I get ready. First, though, I gotta make sure I'mma be okay with everything. And I think I know just what I'mma have to do."

"What?" Reese asked, sensing how her girl Desirae had gotten so serious toward the end of what she'd just said. "What you mean by that, Desirae?"

Desirae looked dead into Reese's face then glanced down at her own stomach. "I'mma have to get that nigga on board," Desirae said. "Even if I do get on my mama's insurance, I can't sit up and ask her to take care of me. Me and you both know that ain't no job gon hire me knowing that I'm pregnant. This is Tron's baby…hmmhmm…and he got plenty of free time now to help me take of it. I'm not gon' give him no other choice."

16

Chapter 2

"Man, I don't know why the fuck you would even think that is a good idea," Tron said. "I don't think getting rid of any of the girls is the way to go with this shit, bruh. I really don't."

"Think about it," Tyrese reasoned. "If we get more girls up in there, we can draw more niggas. Draw more niggas, and they buying more drinks and shit. You said you want an edge. Man, I say it's time to go up a notch with your shit."

Tyrese and Tron sat across from one another at the dining room table at Tron's townhouse. Tyrese was staying with Tron at this point, and at times it was a little difficult for Tron. Sure, Tyrese had been his boy since the two of them were teenagers. Furthermore, they dipped in and out of that street life—just enough to make some money, and now owned a strip club together. At the same time, though, that didn't mean that Tron wanted to come home and live with the dude too. Now, instead of meeting up at the club or wherever to talk business, it could happen at any point.

For the last few hours, Tyrese had really been on one. Even with all the snow outside, he managed to get two chicks to be on their way over. Roughly an hour or so before the girls were due to show up, the two of them had fallen into a conversation about how to remodel the front of the club so that it would not be recognizable from being on the news.

"Dude, I agree that we need to prolly change the look of the club altogether," Tyrese said. "And I think if we got more hoes up in there, it would really become a place niggas can come and chill. Even more than that, you know what I always said we should do."

"Nigga, we not pimps," Tron said. "So I don't even know why you bringin' that shit up."

"You know they gon be doing that shit already," Tyrese said. "We might as well figure out a way to get in on it so we benefitting from it too."

Tron shook head, not wanting to give in to the idea that he was thinking about Tyrese's idea about how to make up some of the money they would be spending on a remodel. For the last few months, Tyrese had wanted to look the other way when the dancers would do sexual favors for the dudes that came into the club.

"Man, them rooms we got in the back," Tyrese said, moving his hands about as he sat across from Tron, who was thinking seriously about what he had to say. "You know how many of them married niggas and shit would come off a little money to use one of them rooms with the girls, basically any fuckin' time they want to bust a nut."

"Nigga, that is the last thing we need to be on the news for," Tron said. "Prostitution and shit."

"Nigga, we not sellin' the pussy," Tyrese said. "We sellin' the space where the niggas get the pussy. There is a difference. Fuck, they could go up in there and give them dudes hand jobs for all we know."

"But we know they not just gon be jackin' they shit off for'em," Tron said.

Tyrese shook his head. "Maybe you know that," he said. "But I don't know that. I'm not gon be in there with them. Plus, we could keep it exclusive."

"Exclusive?" Tron said. "What the fuck you mean *exclusive*?"

"Do this shit in such a way that only the real niggas, like Lime and Ryan and that nigga from out west, Donny and them kinda niggas," Tyrese said. "You know they got wifeys and shit, but they need a little somethin' on the side."

There was no doubt about that in Tron's mind. However, letting the girls fuck dudes who were dropping a little cash to use a room in the back just did not sit all that well with him. At this point, he was so fearful of being on the news for something else that he almost wanted to get into the church business.

"Man, let's just talk about this shit tomorrow," Tyrese said, leaning back in his chair. "We got a couple of hoes coming over, and your ass know that you need that shit."

Tron smirked. He had woken up this morning with a hard dick and some crazy thoughts going through his mind. At the same time, though, for days he had been thinking about what went down with Shawna and Desirae. At first, he had sort of assumed that after a few days, it wouldn't seem so real to him because he would have had some time to think about. He found that he was wrong. Now, it had been about three days since he'd seen either of them and he still felt so out of control with the entire situation.

"Yeah, yeah, nigga," Tron said. "When they gon' be gettin here?"

Tyrese looked at his phone, his text messages. "Ronnicha, the one with the big ole ass," he said, smiling. "She said that they gon leave out at about nine or so and head this way."

"And this other chick?" Tron asked. "Who she?"

"This thot too, basically, nigga," Tyrese said. "She bad, though. I give her that. She thick and shit, alright in the face. That mouth, though."

"Oh yeah?" Tron asked.

"Hell yeah?" Tyrese said. "I ain't never had none, myself. But even her girl Ronnicha was telling me that her bedroom door during the day…let's just say the bitch gets plenty of practice suckin' dick."

Tron shook his head and stood up. "Man, I don't know," he said. "I mean, I got a lot on my mind."

"Nigga, I know you do," Tyrese said. "And ain't shit wrong with that. That's exactly why we got a couple of hoes comin' over to chill for a minute…a little while, so you can chill the fuck out."

Just as Tron was about to say something, Tyrese cut him off.

"And nigga, you ain't gotta worry about them holding you hostage or no shit like that," Tyrese said, playfully. "I'mma keep you safe."

Tron looked at his boy Tyrese, immediately thinking back to just a few days ago when he had gotten out of the shower and found the two chicks in his life standing in the doorway of his bedroom.

"Nigga, whatever," Tron said. "You let them bitches come up in here and ambush me."

"Man, we been over this shit," Tyrese said. "I told you I ain't let them do shit. Shawna, as you know since you ain't changed the locks or nothin', still got a key. I just happened to be walking out to my car when they came up and were going in the door."

"And you couldn't let a nigga know or no shit?" Tron asked.

"Man, I was try'na think of ways to do that," Tyrese said. "But I couldn't think of shit that wouldn't be too obvious. Plus, they was already in here when I was just getting into my trunk to get the little broom off. You know we had all that damn snow."

"Yeah, well," Tron said. "It wasn't enough to stop'em from coming up in here like that and jumping on me."

"All the more reason you need to just move the fuck on from that shit, man," Tyrese said, wanting his boy Tron to go back to the single life. "Remember when we both was single and how simple life was? You remember that shit? We hopped in the car and went wherever, whenever we wanted without nobody breathin' down our necks and shit."

"Nigga, I wasn't whooped like your ass," Tron said, almost laughing. "You already know you wouldn't be talkin' that shit if Nalique was here. She get that ass in line."

"Man, whatever," Tyrese said, looking away. "Nalique ain't control me, I controlled her."

"Sure," Tron said, sarcastically. "Your ass was running from her last I saw."

"Wasn't you the one that got cornered without no damn clothes on in your own fuckin' house?" Tyrese said. "I mean, bruh, come on. They both jumped on you and got in that ass. You still got a couple scratches and bumps on you, nigga."

"Nigga, fuck you," Tron said, shaking his head. "But, for real, though. I don't know if I feel like no hoes tonight."

"Okay, okay," Tyrese said, thinking of a way that his boy's indecisiveness could work in his favor. "If you ain't feelin' the shit when they get here and shit, I'll take'em both while you in your feelings and shit."

"Nigga, whatever," Tron said. "You can't handle both of them."

Just then, Tyrese's phone vibrated against the surface of the dining room table. He picked it up and saw that it was text message from Ronnicha: *We on the way.*

"Aight, bruh," Tyrese said. "They leaving out."

Tyrese looked around quickly, being sure that the place was still together and stuff. Earlier, he had gone out and bought a quarter-ounce of some smoke. It sat out on the dining room table, at the other end from where he and Tron stood. A couple bottles were chilling in the refrigerator, in case they wanted to use them.

Tyrese looked at Tron, being able to clearly tell that he was thinking about something. "Nigga, I know what your problem is," he said. "You just need to smoke and be coo."

The two of them chilled out for a minute while they waited on Ronnicha and her girl, Gracelyn, to come pulling up. It wasn't long before Tyrese was getting a text message that they were outside. He went and opened the door. He hugged them both while

20

Tron came into the room. Tron's eyes immediately dropped to both of the girls' bodies. They were thick in all of the right places with flat stomachs and hips that even stuck out under their coats. *Damn, Tyrese wasn't lying*, Tron thought.

"This my nigga, Tron," Tyrese said, introducing the two chicks to him as they took their coats off and threw them over the staircase banister. "This Ronnicha and Gracelyn."

Tron smiled, not being able to help himself from looking both females up and down. He could feel their eyes looking at him, for several seconds too long. Next thing they knew, Tyrese was moving the party into the living room. Tron followed both girls into the living, enjoying the sight in front of him as each of them had ass cheeks that bounced with every step they took.

"Nice place," Ronnicha said.

"Thank you," Tron responded. "We try to keep it clean and all between being so busy, but yeah…it's cool."

Tron, Gracelyn, and Ronnicha all sat on the couch while Tyrese grabbed the smoke off of the table. Tron, meanwhile, could feel Gracelyn's eyes looking him up and down. It was obvious that she liked what she saw and wasn't afraid to let him know it. Tron, liking the attention, and now seeing that Gracelyn had some fat lips, simply smiled back and tried to be cool with it.

"So, ladies," Tyrese said. "Do the two of you smoke?"

"Fuck yeah," Gracelyn said.

"Hmm…hmm," Ronnicha said, nodding her head. "That shit gets a girl feelin' good."

"I know, don't it," Gracelyn said, showing that she had a bit of an accent in her voice.

Tron noticed Gracelyn's accent. "You from Nap or?" he asked.

Gracelyn smiled and shook her head. "Naw, not originally, no," she answered. "I was born in St. Louis, then we lived in Arkansas for a little bit, then moved up north, up here. I got family here."

"That's wassup," Tron said, nodding. He then made eye contact with Tyrese, whose eyes practically glistened at the sight of a couple of thick chicks sitting over on the couch. The girls giggled and said something or another to one another while Tron got up and went over to the table.

21

"Damn, nigga," Tron said. "Takin' you longer than usual to roll that shit up, huh?"

"Nigga, you see they ass?" Tyrese asked, shaking his head. "Got damn."

"Yeah," Tron said. "They over there holding. That is for sure."

"Man, this shit gon be so good," Tyrese said as he licked the blunt to seal it. "This some of that good shit too, and they got ass for days over there. Nigga, I'mma fuck the shit outta one of them to the point where they not gon be able to walk out of here."

"Who said we would wanna walk outta here?" Ronnicha asked, smiling.

Just then, Tyrese and Tron looked over to the couch and saw Ronnicha and Gracelyn looking straight at them. Ronnicha was looking into Tyrese's eyes while Gracelyn looked at Tron. Tron and Tyrese then turned and looked at each other before grabbing the blunt and the lighter and going back over to the couch.

The four of them talked while they passed a blunt around. After a while, especially once Tron was feeling the weed, he was able to chill out much better than he had been earlier. Sure, Shawna and Desirae were on his mind, but he put that shit to the back of his mind and just focused on the couple of thick chicks that were sitting right there in front of him.

"So, Tron?" Gracelyn asked, putting her hand on his leg. "You alright over here?"

At this point, Tyrese and Ronnicha were really just focusing on each other more than conversation as an entire group.

Tron nodded. "Hell yeah," he said, calmly. "You alright?"

Gracelyn, who Tron was seeing looked a lot like a really thick version of Meagan Good, smiled and shrugged her shoulders. "I'm good, I guess," she answered. "I mean, you know how a bitch is feeling. That weed is some good shit."

Tron smiled, admitting in his mind that his boy Tyrese could always get ahold of some good stuff to smoke. If he couldn't do anything else, he could definitely be Mr. Social to get the good stuff.

"Yeah, he always got the hookup," Tron said. "And yeah, this shit got me feelin' good."

Tron lay his head back onto the back of the couch and smiled. "Fuck," he said, not realizing that it had slipped out of his mouth. He started to feel his dick starting to get hard a little while Gracelyn's hand moved up and down his thigh.

"You sure you alright over there?" Gracelyn asked, trying to seem as attentive as possible.

Tron looked back down at this twenty-something year old sitting next to him. Without even realizing it, his eyes dropped down to her ass again. The way it splayed out from her hips as she sat drove him crazy. In a swift move, he slid his arm down from being on the back of the couch. Before Gracelyn knew it, Tron's arm hand was on the other side of her body. She closed her eyes and enjoyed the brief feeling of his hand grabbing her hip.

Tron smiled. "Yeah, I'm good," he said. "Just been stressed and shit lately. A lot goin' on."

Just then, Tron felt Gracelyn move her hand more toward his fly while she never broke eye contact with him for one second. She smiled.

"Oh, yeah?" Gracelyn said, wanting to know more.

Tron licked his lips and lightly shrugged his shoulders. He knew that he would be a fool to pass on at least getting some mouth. Even when he was high on that good stuff, he could see the real deal about everything. This chick was just sitting on too much ass for him to pass up on the opportunity.

Tron and Gracelyn glanced over at Tyrese and Ronnicha on the other end of the sectional couch. Tyrese's head was put back and he bit his lip. Ronnicha's head went up and down in his lap, with a constant slurping noise.

Just as Tron was about to say something to Gracelyn, her head too was heading down toward his lap. Her small hands undid his belt buckled then zipper and she pulled out his soft dick and began to suck on it. Before long, Tron's manhood had gotten to its full size.

"Shit nigga," Gracelyn said.

Tron, not really paying attention to Gracelyn, looked down at her for the first time since she had gotten his pants undone. For whatever reason, of which he did not know, he immediately started to compare Gracelyn to Desirae. Gracelyn only got a couple of inches past the head of his dick while Desirae could go all the way down. Shawna had a wetter mouth overall. Tron glanced around the room, over at his boy Tyrese getting into what he was feeling. Just then, for so many seconds, Tron zoned out. Desirae being pregnant rushed through his mind then Shawna being broken hearted – two things that killed his hard-on right away. The two of them meeting each other and coming and jumping on him like they did still was fresh on his mind.

Next thing Tron knew, he just wasn't feeling getting with some hoe like this. As hard as he tried, he just could not ignore everything he had going. This may have been what Tyrese was trying to do, but Tron knew that he had far too much on his mind to be doing all of this right now. He began to lift up, causing Gracelyn to choke for a split second.

"Watch out, watch out," he said to her.

Gracelyn pulled her head up and wiped her forearm across her mouth. "What's wrong?" she asked, almost feeling insulted that Tron would get up while she was down on him. "Huh, Tron?"

"Nothing," Tron said as he put himself back together, buckling his belt and whatnot. "It ain't you, it's me. It ain't you. I just got a lotta shit on my mind is all, like I told you. A lot of shit."

Gracelyn reached for Tron's crotch, telling him that she could help him relax. Tron, now seeing her as only a mouth, swatted her away.

"Naw, not right now," he said, in a very unconcerned way. "I can't do this shit right now."

By now, Ronnicha had pulled her head up as she and Tyrese were looking. The look on Tyrese's face made it clear to everyone in the room that he was confused.

"Aye, nigga," Tyrese said. "What the fuck is up with you?"

"I'mma go step out for a second," Tron said. He then walked over to the dining room area, grabbed his coat off of the back of a chair, and slid into it. Never, for one second, did he look into anyone's eyes in the room. He simply walked out of the front door.

"What the fuck was up with that nigga?" Gracelyn asked.

Tyrese shrugged, seeing that Ronnicha was looking up to him for some sort of explanation. "Fuck if I know," Tyrese said. "Come over here, sexy. I got enough for the two of you to share."

Ronnicha smiled. "This shit is big as fuck, girl," she said.

Gracelyn went over to the other side of the section. Tyrese's head leaned back while either hand was on each girl's head.

***

24

"Fuck!" Tron said, to himself. "I got a fuckin' baby on the way."

Even though there was a good seven inches of snow out on the ground, Tron felt ten times better out in it then in the house with Tyrese and those chicks. The second he walked out of the door, he felt silly for even thinking that he would be in the mood to entertain, so to speak.

"This is some fucked up shit," Tron said to himself. "Don't fuckin' believe this shit."

Even with talking to Desirae about it all and her seeming as if she really didn't plan this, Tron could not help but see the opposite. The more he thought about it, the more he thought of how he'd fallen for the oldest trick in the book – the trick that got every older nigga back in the day in his family. And, now? Now, even though he had worked so hard to have a little something, he still managed to get caught up in some baby-mama shit.

"But maybe it ain't mine," he said.

Tron paused for a moment when he came to the community space between two buildings. There, covered in snow, were picnic tables and a jungle gym-type structure. Tron walked over to the picnic table and walked in circles around it for a couple of minutes. He knew that thinking that the baby Desirae was carrying was not his was a fantasy. On the flip side of that, though, he knew that for his own sake he would be better safe than sorry just to be sure that the baby was his. So what if Desirae didn't like it that he asked for a paternity test? Chicks do it to dudes all the time and everything is cool. Plus, Tron just had to be sure. Before he lived up to any possible responsibilities, he wanted to be sure that the responsibilities are indeed his. If there was one thing that he had learned in life is just how rare it is that a side chick will be loyal. Who knew how many other dudes Desirae was fucking around with?

Chapter 3

These three days had been a few long salty days for Shawna. Everything that had happened with Tron, and her going to jail over some bullshit like that when she was just defending herself, was just too much to think about. Sure, she felt lucky that the judge let the both of them go. She knew that since she was the one who came up in the store and looked for the chick that she would definitely look like the one who started it all. Shawna shook her head. "If only they knew," she said.

"Yeah, I can understand how you feeling," Ms. Susan said.

Shawna spent this particular evening at the shop. Ms. Susan had sent her a text message asking her if she could squeeze in a quick touch-up so she could look good for some man she was going to be hooking up with the next day. Because she wouldn't have time the next day, she made sure to get with Shawna as early as she could that day to see when and if she could squeeze her in. Little did Ms. Susan know, Shawna always tried her hardest to make time to squeeze her in.

"Girl, I'm sorry you had to go to jail over that shit," Ms. Susan said. "Excuse me…my language. But now you done learned. The two of y'all stopped being stupid and went and jumped on that nigga like a couple bad bitches, huh?"

Shawna tapped Ms. Susan's shoulder. "Miss Susan," she said, smiling. "Don't make it sound like that."

"I'm just calling it how I see it, Shawna," Ms. Susan said. "I mean, don't take it the wrong way. I been there just like you. Hell…" Susan looked into the mirror, loving how her hair was looking so good. "And I'm kinda there again if I say so myself."

While working on her hair, seeing all of the new growth on the back of her neck, Shawna squinted. She didn't know what Ms. Susan meant by that, but wasn't going to give it that much thought.

"So, Miss Susan," Shawna said. "Now that I done told you about what's been going on with me, tell me what you up to. We been talking about me and my fiasco since you pulled into the parking lot."

"Girl, it ain't no problem with me," Susan said. "I live through my young people. How you think your girl stay looking so good like I do? I don't hang out with people my age. They be boring and ain't nobody got time to be bored."

"I know that's right," Shawna said, snickering at how Ms. Susan was always one to keep it real. That was the very reason Shawna never hesitated to tell Ms. Susan what was going on in her life. She always felt like she really learned a little something from Ms. Susan and her experiences, especially with how she treated her life like it was an open book. It was just so rare to find someone as cool and real as her. "So, spill," Shawna said, wanting to know about the guy Ms. Susan would be going to meet. "Who got you running out in a foot of snow to meet them?"

Ms. Susan looked into Shawna's eyes through the mirror, grinning. She then looked down.

"Miss Susan?" Shawna insisted.

"Well, this guy I met," Susan said.

"I know you met him, Miss Susan," Shawna said. "So, tell me about him and stuff. Where did you meet him? What he do? Fill me in a little. Must be something if you going through all this."

"He just said that he would be picking me up when he get off the highway tomorrow from work and I wanna be sure I'm looking good as possible after a long day of dealing with them white people," Susan said. "Fuck, why I say that? Excuse me…my language."

"When he gets off the highway?" Shawna asked, smiling. "Okay, so it sound to me like you done went out and got you a truck driver."

"Naw, girl," Susan said. "He don't drive no truck, not exactly."

"Not exactly?" Shawna asked.

"Well, damn, you really want to hear about this don't you?" Susan asked, remembering her younger self and how intrigued she was, too, in the love life of older women she knew. She would always remember her aunt "dating" after her divorce. It was always so awkward to her and now she felt as if she was in that aunt's shoes, in so many ways. "Okay, I'll tell you," Susan said. "He live over in Dayton."

"Dayton?" Shawn asked, surprised. "How did you meet some dude in Ohio, Miss Susan?"

"We met here, but he live in Dayton," Susan explained.

"So y'all gon try the semi-long distance thing for a little while and then maybe he move here?" Shawna asked. "I mean, ain't shit… excuse me, my language… stuff in Dayton. He might as well gon head and move here."

"Well, it ain't that simple," Susan explained, not believing that she was about to open up. At the same time, she felt it was necessary because she could see by what Shawna had been going through with Tron and his other chick that Shawna had some things to still pick up on. "When he free and stuff, he gon come to Indy and see me and stuff."

Shawna was starting to get a bad feeling. Something just didn't feel right with what Ms. Susan was telling her. Why would he be cool with just living in Dayton and coming to see her when he "got some time."

"So, how often might that be?" Shawna asked, wanting to clarify whatever fogginess she was having about how Ms. Susan had met this man and what would be the nature of their relationship.

"I don't know, girl," Ms. Susan answered. "He's…" She hesitated before forcing it out. "Shawna, baby, if I tell you this, you gotta promise you not gon look at me like I'm a bad person or something."

"Miss Susan," Shawna said. "I'm not a kid anymore. I can take stuff for what it is and…"

"He's married," Susan said.

Shawna stopped what she was doing and looked into the mirror, into Susan's face.

"Goddammit, I knew you was gon' look at me like that, Shawna," Susan said. "Excuse me…my language. I knew I shouldn't have told you, Shawna, but I knew that with all you was telling me, it would only be right."

"So, what, Ms. Susan," Shawna asked, in a bit of a stern voice as she went back to Susan's hair. "So, like, is this dude separated or something?"

There was a long pause where Susan didn't answer. Shawna picked up on it. "Miss Susan?" she asked again.

"Well, not exactly," Susan said. "Not that I know of. You see, he travels. He travels for his job and he comes to Indianapolis on a regular basis for some project or something. Oh, baby, you know that Indianapolis and Dayton ain't nothing apart. You can probably stand on top of the Chase Tower downtown and see Dayton from here."

"That ain't the point," Shawna said. "Don't give me no geography class, Miss Susan. So, he not separated from his wife. It sound to me like you just gon' be his little piece of…"

"Girl, watch your language," Susan said. "A lady doesn't talk that way."

"Something to do," Shawna finished, knowing that she needed to come up with something that would be smooth yet appropriate.

Susan hesitated. "Not exactly."

Shawna smirked. "Then, what exactly?"

"We just gon enjoy each other's company and, you know," Susan said.

Shawna nodded, just wanting to allow the conversation to die. She had never been a side chick, that she knew of, in her life. The idea of being a man's something else to do when he gets bored with what he already has at home just did not sit well with Shawna. If nothing else, she had always thought of herself as a respectful kind of girl who was not going to go around stealing men from other women. Furthermore, now that she was the man's woman in the situation, she could not deny the fact that she was starting to see Ms. Susan in a different way. What it all boiled down to was the fact that she just could not see Ms. Susan being okay with being the side chick. Shawna just wished that she had never asked.

The two of them chatted about some other things for the rest of the time Susan sat in Shawna's chair. Shawna simply tried to put it out of her mind. When Ms. Susan got up, paid her, and walked out of the front door, Shawna sat in her chair. Her chair was quickly becoming the one spot, especially in the middle of the night when it was just her in the shop, where she would sit and reflect on things.

Ever since finding out that Tron was having a baby by Desirae, Shawna was not comfortable with her own feelings. The fact of the matter is that she hated how she still felt like she loved him even though he fucked around on her and even went ss far as getting the chick pregnant. Soon after thinking about this, Shawna started to shake her head. She thought about going to jail over fighting his other chick and immediately felt so embarrassed. She didn't regret going over there and jumping on him, because that was what Tron deserved. It all was just so confusing to her, simply because two weeks or so ago, they were a happy couple. She had even thrown him a birthday party when he came back into town from Louisville that day. It made her mad to think about how she'd found out that he'd really gotten back to Indianapolis the night before and spent the night over at the chick's place. Shawna had to keep it real with herself, though. It really wasn't the fact that Tron had cheated on her. She felt like she could overlook cheating and continue on with the relationship in some way. However, what bothered her the most was the fact that Tron was so invested in the chick, and he did it all secretly – practically having two worlds that he thought would never meet.

Shawna shook her head as she cleaned up her area and grabbed her keys to head back to her sister Morgan's place.

"This just don't make no sense," Shawna said to herself, as she turned off the lights in the salon.

Chapter 4

Desirae got up the next day, finding it weird that she didn't have a job to go to later on in the afternoon. It was the first time since she was a teenager that she had gotten her day started without having a job to go to at some point in the day. She took her time getting out of bed, even making some tea with lemon. Getting everything off of her chest to Reese really did help a lot last night. Now, Desirae felt like she had stripped away all of the bullshit about the situation and could carry on with thinking about the practical. She was starting to realize that her feelings didn't matter. She was going to have to figure out what she was going to do about her life. Having a baby on the way mixed with no job just did not go together. The more Desirae thought about it, the more she felt nervous and even scared. And Desirae knew that she'd never been the kind of girl to find anything in life scary. However, this was not just anything. She looked down at her stomach as she drank her tea. *In nine months*, she thought. *I'm gonna be getting up in the middle of the night and changing diapers. Who would have ever thought?*

The snow was still standing rather tall on the roofs of cars and nearby houses. However, the parking lot had been plowed and she could see cars moving at a pretty decent speed down Thompson Road. All the signs, as well as the gut feelings that she just could not ignore, were telling her that today would be the day she could roll over to see her mama. She kept trying to figure out how her mother might react, but after a while she realized that with her mother, there was no guessing how she was going to react. The fact of the matter was that there has never been and will never be a formula for predicting her mother's actions, let alone the words that were going to come out of her mouth. Her mother just kept it real and did so at all times.

Desirae grabbed her cell phone off of the couch, looked through her contacts, and tapped Mom. She waited for her to answer.

"Hello?"

"Mama?" Desirae said. "What you doing?"

"It's what *are* you doing," her mother, Karen, corrected her. "And I'm actually just walking in the door. I went in to work for just a half-day and decided to come on home. I think I heard that we might be getting some more snow later on this afternoon. You know

I don't too much care for dealing with that traffic downtown when it snows if I really don't have to."

"Yeah, I know," Desirae said, starting to feel really hesitant about calling her mother.

"What's wrong, Desirae?" Karen asked. "I can hear it in your voice."

Desirae took a deep breath. There was so much wrong no matter how she looked at it that she just could not think of a way to answer that question.

"Mama," she said. "I was calling to see if I could come over in a little bit and talk to you."

"Of course you can, Desirae," Karen said. "I'm not going anywhere. You haven't lost your key, have you?"

"Naw, I still got it," Desirae told her.

"Alright," Karen said. "Just come over when you get ready. And please, slow down. Some streets are really a mess."

"Okay, see you in a minute," Desirae said.

The two said bye to one another and Desirae felt her heart jump. It was already bad enough to her mother that she wasn't going to college, or at least not right away. Her mother had been a teacher for twenty-something years then transitioned into social work. Desirae, at times, felt like she was already letting her mother down because she did not think that college was right for her. She knew that telling her mother she was pregnant by some nigga she hasn't been introduced to was really going to start something. Desirae could feel it. The skies outside may have been sunny, but Desirae felt very dark inside.

***

Desirae's mother, Karen, lived in a small house, in a nice area of Indianapolis. Desirae didn't grow up there, though. Rather, when she was a child, she came home to a mother and father as her parents had been married for fifteen years. After the divorce when she was a teenager, her father wound up moving to Ft. Wayne. He had remarried and everything – a whole new family in all reality. She still was close to him and he came down and visited her often. At this moment, when she pulled up at her mother's house, she didn't even want to think about the conversation she'd be having when she called her father and told him. Her father wasn't what people would call overprotective of his daughter, but he would tell her what he really thought and how he felt just so she would understand. For now, though, Desirae only had to deal with her mother, and it was even more important because her mother would probably be the one helping her because she lived nearby.

When Desirae walked into her mother's house, wearing some cute jeans that showed her shape nicely and a white sweater, she found her mother in the kitchen.

"Hey Mama," Desirae said, looking at the back of her mother, who looked a lot like Angela Basset. Her mother was somewhat tall, and had always been thin with a little bit of a shape. Desirae loved how her mother had been rocking a pixy cut for as long as she could remember, but always got her hair done in such a way that the style never really looked the same twice. She was still in her beige pants suit, clearly not having changed since she'd gotten home about an hour and a half ago.

"Hey, Desirae," Karen said. She then turned around and grinned. "You look....cute."

Desirae smiled. "I knew you would love it," she said, sarcastically because it was obvious that her mother didn't approve of what she was wearing. This was nothing new, though.

"So that's what took you so long to get over here, huh?" Karen said. "You had to do that jump up and down thing to get into them pants."

Desirae rolled her eyes and walked around the kitchen table to a chair. "Whatever, Mama," she said.

"Don't whatever me," Karen said. "Girl, I have told you about what you wear and how you present yourself to the world. It makes a difference with how you are perceived and whatnot. I just wish you would understand that, Desirae."

"I do, Mama," Desirae said, wanting to just get all of this over with. "I really do. So, anyway, I came here for a reason other than how cute I look."

"Cute?" Karen asked, smirking as she turned around. "Alright, Desirae. If that's what you think. So what's up? What is going on with you? You don't seem your usual self like when you were over here last week and the week before that. Haven't seen you in church, either, for that matter."

"I told you I will get back into the steady church thing when I'm ready, Mama," Desirae said.

"Yeah," Karen said. "It's hard getting up to be on time to church when you were out at the club all night the night before until five in the morning, doing that twerking business."

"Anyway," Desirae said, gripping the table with the palms of her hand at this point. "I'm pregnant."

Just then, Desirae saw her mother's head drop down and shake side to side.

***

Tron waited to come back into the apartment last night until it was well after three in the morning. He wound up going for a ride in his car when he couldn't take being outside in the cold anymore. Strangely enough, he found it relaxing to ride around downtown in the snow and middle of the night. Everything was so calm and peaceful. The parks were covered in fresh white snow. He just drove around for a good hour before going to get something to eat at a Steak 'n Shake. He wound up sitting in the restaurant for a little while, thinking about how the last thing he wanted right then was to have a child on the way with Desirae. Losing Shawna was just the cherry on top that he couldn't ignore either.

When Tron got back to his place, Tyrese was passed out with both Gracelyn and Ronnicha sprawled out on the floor next to him. They lay on top of a sheet while the first floor of the townhouse smelled of marijuana. Tron shook his head and went upstairs. He found some humor in knowing how much fun Tyrese had while he was out. Two chicks with thick, fat asses probably caused his boy to have a heart attack.

Tron woke up today with business on his mind initially. He wanted to make sure that he did whatever possible to save the club. The location was perfect, even if there had been some issues. The building was the right size and cost the right price. Furthermore, they had started the business off of drug money they had saved up. In Tron's eyes, there was just no way that either of them would be able to save that kind of money again without having to get back out into the street. And doing that was the very thing that he was trying to avoid at all costs. That life was behind him, for Tyrese, too, for that matter, and he preferred that it stayed that way.

Once Tron got ready and got his clothes on to really get his day started, his phone started ringing. When he looked at the screen, he saw that it was a 502 number – Louisville – and that it looked familiar. He answered.

"Hello."

"Hello, Tron," the woman's voice said.

"Who this?" Tron asked, not liking when he was on the phone talking with someone whose voice he didn't recognize.

"What you mean who this?" the woman asked. "It's Andria."

At that moment, Tron wanted to scream out the word *fuck* – scream it as loud as he possibly could. Andria was his ex, who lived down in Louisville with their daughter. They had a cool relationship now and stuff, but he really didn't feel like dealing with whatever she was calling about. Today was just not the day for him. However, he went ahead and took a deep breath and remembered that he had to be the person to take the high road, for the sake of his daughter and his time going in and out of the court system. Andria could be a little childish and get really stuck in her feelings. She was a pretty good mother and didn't keep Tron from seeing his daughter, but sometimes she could really get into a mood over petty stuff. That was one thing Tron didn't like when they had been together for a good year or so back when they were much younger.

"Oh, Andria," Tron said. "Wassup? How you?"

"I'm good, thanks for asking," Andria said. "I'm surprised you didn't know my voice."

"I mean, Ebony is old enough now," Tron explained. "That I just get used to hearing her voice when I call and stuff. Just kind of caught me off guard is all. Wassup?"

"Hmm, hmm," Andria said.

The only thing Tron missed about Andria at this point was her sexy voice. It sounded so smooth – not too high, not too low. And it was even better through the phone.

"So, you know her birthday is coming up in a couple of weeks, right?" Andria asked.

"Of course," Tron said, knowing that his daughter's birthday had been the farthest thing from his mind in the last couple of days. With what was going on with the club, his relationship, and his side chick, he simply had not had a moment to even think about Ebony's birthday. So much was happening with him that the thought of two weeks from now was just so distant. "The sixteenth, I know," he said. "Wassup, though? That's two weeks and some from now."

35

"I know, Tron," Andria said. "But I was thinking we get a jump on this. I was thinking we do something special since the last couple of birthdays you couldn't come down."

"I feel you on that," Tron said, liking the idea. "But, I mean, what did you have in mind? You know how her birthday be at the worst time of the year, in the middle of February. We can't even really plan anything for her birthday because we don't know what kinda weather problems there might be."

"I know, I know," Andria said. "That's why I was thinking."

Tron knew what was about to come out of Andria's mouth. Deep down, he always felt like Andria still had a thing for him even though they'd been broken up for so long. She was cool with Shawna, mainly because Shawna was so mature acting compared to a lot of chicks her age.

However, even Shawna thought that some of the things Andria called asking for were just ways to get and stay a little closer to him. He never thought that Andria saw it as enough by having his child. It was like she always wanted more and really had a hard time letting go after they broke up.

"I was thinking, Tron, that maybe we take her somewhere warm to where we ain't got to worry about the snow and stuff," Andria said.

Tron shook her head and took a deep breath before talking into the phone. "Andria, not right now," he said. "I got too much going right now to be taking trips and stuff."

"Oh, really," Andria said. "Not even for your daughter, Tron? Damn, she saw her daddy more when he was a drug dealer than she does now he's a business man…wannabe."

Tron bit his bottom lip, hating how Andria would say little antagonizing things.

"Business is," Tron started to say, knowing that he was about to tell a lie. No matter what, he always made sure to keep Andria thinking a certain thing. He was lucky enough to work a deal out with her where he paid the child support straight to her rather than going through the court system. And for that, Tron truly was grateful…especially now, since he had gotten Desirae pregnant and she was definitely the kind of woman to get that kind of shit started even if he was willing to work with her. "It's going good, Andria. Just right now with what all is going on with business and my family

36

down there, as you know, I really can't be taking no trips nowhere just for her birthday."

"Look, Tron," Andria said. "I know, I know. But look, she wants to go somewhere. She so tired of being in Louisville, so I was thinking that maybe she would come spend the weekend up there or something. You can take her to the Children's Museum or something up there just so she can get a change or something. Plus, you know she like your new chick, Shawna."

Tron shook his head, feeling the wound on the situation open just a little. He knew that he definitely wasn't going to tell Andria what had happened. He hadn't even told his own family, like his mother or siblings, that they broke up. On top of that, he knew that sooner or later he was going to have to tell his family that he had a baby on the way. The difference with Desirae versus Andria is that his family at least knew Andria back when the two of them were together. Desirae was really just something that looks good and would open those legs. Tron definitely never meant to have a child by her. Furthermore, if he wanted his two children to have a relationship, then Desirae and Andria would eventually have to meet one another. And Tron knew that with how Desirae acted and approached every situation, there was definitely going to be some fireworks coming about in a situation where Tron simply didn't need any more surprises.

"I don't know," Tron said, to the idea of his daughter coming up to Indianapolis to spend the weekend. "You know we getting our asses beat with this snow, and it probably ain't gon get no better for at least a few weeks."

"Yeah, but that's why I'm saying if…" Andria said. "If the weather is okay and stuff, do you think you can do that? When you at the club working and stuff, maybe you could get Shawna to chill with her a little bit and stuff. You know I don't have no problem with Shawna, and I really hope I ain't never gave her that kind of impression that would mislead her to think that I do. I mean, you know last time I saw her, I felt like she was a little cold toward me, but I wasn't gon' say nothing."

Tron decided that he just needed to go ahead and let Andria know. Since Shawna wasn't going to be in his life anymore, it would be best if his daughter started to get used to that fact.

"Andria, Andria," Tron said, slowing her sentence down. "We broke up."

There was a brief pause.

"What you mean y'all broke up?" Andria asked. In a way, it sounded to Tron like she was smiling as she said it, but he wasn't going to accuse her. That would start another argument in itself that he just did not feel like dealing with right then.

"Like we are no longer together," Tron said.

"Oh," Andria said, clearly taken aback a little at what she was hearing. "Well, I'm sorry to hear that, Tron. When did that happen?"

"Like a week ago," Tron answered.

"Well," Andria said, clearly trying to figure out what she should say. "I see, so there wouldn't even be nobody to spend time with Ebony if you had to go to the club or anything."

"Not really, no," Tron said.

"Alright," Andria said. "It just all falls on me again. This shit…"

"What you mean this shit?" Tron asked. "You just happened to catch me at a bad time."

"Tron, I think it's something else if you really wanna know what I think," Andria said. "You be try'na act like I don't know you, but I know you. And I really think that this is something else. Any other time, you would be trying to figure out something to do so Ebony ain't let down, especially since you don't get to see her all that often. Now, you say you and Shawna done broke up, and ain't saying much about it. But I swear it seem like it's something else."

"Andria," Tron said, clearly bothered by Andria's tone and how she always looked deeper into things than he wanted her to. "Like I said, me and Shawna broke up and stuff. Plus, my buddy Tyrese staying with me now."

"Well, damn," Andria said. "So what the fuck is really up? I thought he was seeing that butch bitch, whatever her name was. The tall, big one."

"They broke up too," Tron said. "So now he staying over here until he get his own place."

"So, Shawna moved out?" Andria asked, as she was connecting the dots.

Tron hyperventilated, hating how a man is basically at the mercy of a woman when he has a child by her. "Yeah," he said, hesitantly.

"Well," Andria said. "I see. So, what you wanna do? You wanna come down here for her birthday and maybe you can take her to see your mama or something."

"Yeah, let's do that," Tron said. "I mean, if that would be cool with you. Maybe I can take her out of town during the summer or something."

"Yeah, maybe," Andria said. "Well, just text me with what you gon' do. I'mma have a birthday party over here, for the people who find her important enough to come."

"What the fuck is your problem?" Tron asked.

"What you talkin' bout, Tron?" Andria asked. "I ain't got no problem. Everything is gon' be just fine. It wasn't like I expected much more out of you anyway. You always be so damn busy and shit, I don't even know why I bother."

"Andria," Tron started. The phone then cut off. Andria had hung up. Tron clutched his phone tight before tossing it onto the bed while he looked for his hat.

"Man, bitches be on one," he said to himself.

***

Desirae watched as her mother turned around and looked dead into her eyes.

"Pregnant?" Karen asked, clearly not taking the news all that well. "What do you mean you're pregnant?"

Desirae glanced down at her stomach. "Mama, I'm pregnant," she said, realizing that she was going to have to be a grown woman about this situation.

"Since when?" Karen asked, turning the stove off then leaning on the counter with her arms crossed.

"I found out this week," Desirae answered, now looking down. She really hated that she had to tell her mother things, but she knew it would be inevitable.

"Hold up, hold up," Karen said, waving her hands side to side. "How you gon' be pregnant? You aren't even in a relationship with anybody, as far as we know, I guess I should say."

Desirae paused, not really knowing what to say to that.

"Desirae?" Karen asked. "Who are you pregnant by? Please don't tell me the father is one of those thug guys you be running around with and wearing them little tight clothes. Please, don't tell me that."

"Mama, his name is Tron," Desirae said.

"Okay, well what does this Tron say about him having a child on the way?" Karen asked. "Or, please…tell me that you have at least told the man."

Desirae nodded. "Yeah, I did," she said. "I told him."

"And?"

"And what?"

"And what does he think?" Karen asked. "Is he going to step up to his responsibilities or are you just going to be another statistic? Another single, black mother?"

Desirae knew that her mother was going to say something like what she'd just said. It truly was another inevitable thing about this entire situation. To make matters only worse, Desirae didn't know how to answer that question either. She was coming to grips with the fact that there was so much she didn't know about Tron. She really didn't know if he would live up to his responsibilities. She knew that he had a daughter down in Louisville. However, Tron rarely ever even mentioned her.

"Mom, he is the part owner of a club," Desirae said, trying to let her mother know that Tron was at least about something.

"A club?" Karen asked. "Oh God. Well, yeah. Yeah, Desirae. That makes it a whole lot better. Okay, so he owns a club. Let me guess, that's where you met this young man? Up at that club, showing off that body of yours to any and everybody, and hit the jackpot, so to speak, because you got to get with the owner of the place. Hold up. How old is this Tron if he owning a club and stuff?"

"He just a few years older than me, mama," Desirae answered.

"Just a few years older than you?" Karen asked. "And he already own a club and he is just in his mid-twenties." Karen started shaking her head. "I already don't like this situation." Karen turned back around to the stove, clearly not taking this news all that well. "So, what? What is the deal with the two of you? Is this like your boyfriend or something?"

Desirae didn't answer, leading Karen to pick up on the thick silence in her kitchen between her and her daughter.

"Desirae?" Karen asked. "So you weren't even seeing this guy. Hold up, hold up. What happened to your birth control? You know I have to talk to mothers every day almost about the importance of birth control. I know you were on it."

"I was," Desirae said.

"So what happened?" Karen asked.

Desirae stood up. She just did not like where the conversation was going. She truly felt like she was under attack and it was not a good feeling with everything that was going on.

"Okay, I hear your silence," Karen said. "So, you stopped taking your birth control. Desirae, I…I…. I am so disappointed in you. I mean, look at what kind of life you're going to have."

"Mama, I can still make something out of myself, you know," Desirae said. "This ain't the end."

"I know you can," Karen said. "And I didn't say it was the end. But having a baby is a big responsibility. And it's going to be even harder for you since it seem like this baby ain't gon have no daddy."

"Mama, don't say that," Desirae said. "Tron is good."

"But not good enough to date you," Karen said, shutting down this mess. "So, tell me this. How many other baby mothers does Tron have? I know you probably ain't the first to get with the owner of the club."

"He has a daughter down south," Desirae said.

"Down south where?" Karen asked. "What? Atlanta? Alabama? Where down south? This Tron gets around, huh?" Karen shook her head.

"In Louisville," Desirae said. "She's like four or five years old, I think."

"You think?" Karen said. "Desirae, baby, it sounds to me like you really don't know this Tron, and now you're having a baby with him. Be honest with me." Karen looked dead into her daughter's eyes. "Did you do this on purpose?"

"Do what on purpose?" Desirae asked, definitely not liking where this conversation was going. It was one thing for Tron to accuse her of this, but for her mother to do the same when she was supposed to be supportive and whatnot was just getting to be too much.

"You know what I'm talkin' bout, Miss Thang," Karen said. "Did you get pregnant by this nigga on purpose?"

"What the fuck?" Desirae said, clearly angry and without thinking. "What makes you think I would do some shit like that?"

"Girl, you better watch how you talk to me," Karen let Desirae know. "You're not going to be talking to me any old kind of way, even when you are a mother. I am still your mother."

"Naw, you the one who is the problem here," Desirae said. "I can't believe you would even say something like that to me. I mean, what do you think of me."

"Desirae," Karen said, realizing that she probably needed to soften her voice to get her point across to her daughter. "It's not about who I think you are, it's about who I see you acting as. Where is this Tron? Answer me that. Better yet, think about this. You're about to be a mother, right?"

Desirae nodded. "Right."

"Well, imagine if you have a precious little girl," Karen explained. "And she comes walking through your door at twenty-something years old and tells you that she is pregnant by some guy you have never even heard of, let alone seen. How do you think you might feel, Desirae? Use your critical thinking skills."

Desirae could imagine how it all looked.

"Yeah, Mama," she said. "I know."

"Well, I guess I should say Congratulations now, shouldn't I?" Karen asked, smiling. "You're going to be a mother. How do you feel?"

"I don't know how to feel," Desirae said.

"Well," Karen said, setting a couple of plates on the table. "You've got at least seven months to figure it out. Then, once the child gets here, it will be nothing like what you think it is now."

Desirae went ahead and sat back down, realizing that she didn't have anywhere to go anyway.

"So, what did Mister Tron say when you told him?" Karen asked, now much calmer than she had been minutes before.

"I mean," Desirae said, trying to find what she could tell her mother that wouldn't get her going again. "I can tell he wasn't planning for it or anything, you could say."

"Generally, the men aren't," Karen said. "But, I mean, have you really talked to him about it?"

"I told him and he said that he was going to support me no matter what I chose," Desirae said.

"Whatever you choose?" Karen asked. She was now putting spaghetti onto both of their plates and getting bread out of the oven. "You telling me that you were thinking about having an abortion?"

Desirae paused. She had never talked about abortion with her mother, so she didn't know how she was going to respond to that hot topic. For a split second, she tried to think of whether or not her mother had ever said anything about her feelings toward abortion. Nothing was coming to mind.

"No, I wasn't," Desirae said, now feeling like she was getting to the point where she could open up to her mother and really talk to her. "But I think that's what he was wanting."

Karen grumbled under her breath. "Yeah," she said. "I've been there before. I know what that means."

"What'chu mean, Mama?" Desirae asked, picking up on the resentment in her mother's voice. "What'chu mean you've been through this before?"

Karen looked into Desirae's eyes then away. "I was young too, once," she said. "And, believe it or not, I had a life before your father. I wasn't just some princess waiting in a castle for him to come rescue me from eternal loneliness."

"Oh yeah?" Desirae asked, clearly wanting to hear more.

"And I was seeing this guy named James," Karen said. "So, don't get to thinking this story is going to be the same as what you and Mister Tron got going. I was seeing this guy, and my mother and father had met him and everything."

Desirae wondered where this story was going as Karen sat down and they started to eat.

"So, anyway," Karen said, going back in her memory to when she was in her late teens. "James and I were getting kind of serious and, as you can probably guess from how I'm sounding, I got pregnant."

"So, I'm not your first born?" Desirae asked, very surprised. She was surprised that after all these years, her mother had never told her this story.

Karen shook her head. "You're my first born, but not my first pregnancy," she said. "Understand?"

Desirae nodded. "So, what happened?"

"Well," Karen said, sounding a bit hesitant but pushing through it. "I got pregnant when I was eighteen years old and getting ready to go off to college."

Desirae's eyes almost popped out of her head. Karen noticed.

"Be quiet," Karen said, not wanting to hear whatever could possibly be coming out of Desirae's mouth. "And I wound up going to the clinic and getting an abortion. I'm not exactly proud of it, but it was necessary for me and starting my career at the time. I would have a very different life if I had decided to have a baby at just eighteen years old. Some of my girlfriends from the hood did, as did some of my cousins. And you see how their lives are going, don't you?"

Desirae nodded, thinking of her cousins and the few friends she'd met from her mother's past. "Yeah," she said. "So why did you do it? Why did you get an abortion?"

"Well, here is where my story is different from yours," she said. "James wasn't the one who wanted an abortion, actually."

"Really?" Desirae asked.

Karen nodded. "Yes, really," she said. "James, much like this Tron guy, was upset at first that I was pregnant. I swear, they act like they have no idea how that sort of thing happens. But, anyway. Yes, James was okay with it eventually. In fact, he even got to the point where he was looking forward to it."

"So, why?" Desirae asked, seeing the strain in her mother's face at bringing up such an old memory that she clearly wasn't proud of. "Why did you get an abortion, then? Was it your deciding?"

"No, I wouldn't say that," Karen said. "I was even getting to the point where I was looking forward to it, but your grandfather.... Your grandfather talked me into thinking about my career. Plus, he never liked James, so that didn't really help either. He drove a motorcycle, so that made him the enemy to Daddy no matter how he looked at it."

Desirae decided to just remain silent as she thought about how her grandfather had talked her mother into getting an abortion. Her grandfather was always so nice and loving that Desirae just couldn't imagine him trying to do something like that. At the same time, though, Desirae knew that she didn't know him when he was younger. She had already learned in life how much people can change as the age. Here she sat, across from her mother, as she told her about being pregnant at just 18 years old.

"So, what are you saying I should do?" Desirae asked.

"Desirae," Karen said. "I'm not saying that you should do anything. All I'm saying is that I've been where you are, sort of, and I was just letting you know that. You are a bit older than I was at the time, however, so that will make a difference. You'll have to grow up once that baby gets here because that stuff is no joke."

"I already know, Mama," Desirae said. "I already know."

"So, I don't guess that you've called up to your father and told him yet, have you?" Karen asked.

Desirae shook her head. "No," she answered. "I figured I'd just tell you first."

"Well, you know your father is not going to be happy to hear that," Karen said. "But, you'll just have to deal with it and keep on moving, if you are going to keep the baby. I suggest you be deciding those kinds of things as soon as possible so you can work out a budget of sorts and be saving your money."

"Well, that is the other thing," Desirae said to her mother. "About that…"

Karen set her fork down into her plate. "What is another thing, Desirae?" she asked. "You got more news for me."

Desirae hesitated. "I was gon' talk to you about using your health insurance and stuff," Desirae said. "Since I lost my job."

Again, Desirae watched as her mother's head dropped down and she shook it side to side.

"Girl, you have got to be kidding me," Karen said. "How in the hell did you lose your job right when you find out that you're pregnant?"

Chapter 5

When Desirae got home that afternoon after visiting her mother and having something to eat with her, she questioned if she had made the right choice. Sure, she knew that her mother should definitely be among the first people to know that she had a baby on the way. However, Desirae was starting to second guess things. Some of the things her mother had said to her, like about becoming a statistic, really stuck in her mind. In fact, the entire ride home from her mother's house, Desirae progressively saw her situation in a worse light. It would almost seem that with each stoplight she passed through, another thought would come up. Furthermore, all of these thoughts related right back to how unstable of a situation she was in. Desirae just shook her head and told herself that she was going to be all right.

As she walked through the door into her apartment, Desirae gave more thought to her mother's story about having an abortion. She wondered if her mother was trying to tell her something, or could she be overreacting. She even started to wonder the same thing with Tron. After she placed her coat on the back of her dining room chair, she sat down on her couch.

"Fuck," Desirae said, the words slipping out of her mouth. Without even thinking, she began to rub her stomach. Even though she wasn't showing or anything yet, she knew that it would only be a matter of time until she did.

Desirae thought about what her mother said when she told her that she had been fired from Clarke's. Of course, Karen wanted to know how and why she was fired, but Desirae knew that she had to really watch what she told her mother. Some things were okay to tell her, while others should definitely be kept private. She could only imagine what her mother would say if she had told her that she was letting some nigga who already had a girl come over and smash her and wound up pregnant by him. The look on her mother's face said it all – the look said that she did not approve one bit of what Desirae had going on. Desirae knew that she was going to be strong, though. In fact, she even gave herself an imaginary pat on the back for at least going through with telling her mother. She did not expect her mother to go all out and tell her about her past pregnancy, but seeing the softer side of her mother surely did not hurt.

Rather, Desirae started to think, there in the silence of her apartment, about how her mother Karen had asked her if Tron was going to live up to his responsibilities. Desirae had told her mother that she was fired from Clarke's for getting into it with some customer who turned out to be some important person. After her mother gave her a brief lecture on being careful with how you talk to people because you never know who somebody could be, they had gotten back on the topic at hand: her pregnancy and financial situation. She told her mother that she was going to talk to Tron about some things first before she would know if she was going to move back in to the house or not. If Desirae learned anything from tonight, it was that she would do whatever it took to not have to move back in with her mother. She could only imagine having to learn to take care of a newborn baby while her mother was breathing down her neck. It was an uncomfortable situation to even think about.

"Let me go on and call this nigga," Desirae said to herself, referring to Tron. The moment she left her mama's house, she knew that she was going to have to talk to Tron about everything. This was one of those things where sooner would be better than later because she was only sitting on so much money, and she knew that it was only going to last so long. Desirae knew that no matter how she approached the topic with Tron, she had to be smart about it if she wanted him to help her out while she was pregnant with his child. She was sure now that she could use her mother's health insurance, but she was still going to need money to help pay her bills if she didn't want to move back in with her mother.

Desirae grabbed her phone out of her purse and called Tron.

"Hello?" Tron answered.

Desirae took a deep breath, knowing that it had been a few days since the last time she'd seen Tron. In fact, the last time that she had seen him, he was naked in the living room with her and Shawna about to jump on him for the third or fourth time. Even by the way he had said hello when he answered the phone, Desirae could tell that he was probably not in the best of moods.

"Hello, Tron," Desirae said. "How you?"

"What you want, Desirae?" Tron asked sharply. "You know how I'm doin'. So, I don't even know why you call me askin' that shit. What you want?"

Desirae rolled her eyes and shook her head, wondering if this was any way a man should talk to the mother of his child.

"I hope you won't be talking to me like that when the baby comes," Desirae said. "What will the child think if they see Daddy talking to Mommy like that?"

Just then, Desirae could hear Tron grumble under his breath. "I'm fine, Desirae," Tron said. "How are you?"

"Cut out all the formalities," Desirae said. "I just wanted to know when we could get together and have a serious talk about this child. I mean, I know I ain't showing yet or nothin', but I'mma have to get a plan together."

"I know," Tron said, clearly sounding resentful of the matter.

"I mean, if you don't care about this," Desirae said. "Then just let me know. I thought you would be better than that."

"I know, I know," Tron said. "I told you I was gon' be there to support you… Well, support my child. I'm there for the child, no matter what."

Desirae smiled. "Well, that's good," she said. "I mean, that's what a real man supposed to do. So, when you gon' come through so we can get some stuff sorted out. No fighting, I promise. I'mma be on my best behavior so we can really talk about this."

There was a long pause, prompting Desirae to say Tron's name again.

"Yeah, I'm here," Tron said. "I'm just thinking, just thinking. What you doin' in about an hour? When you go into work?"

Work? Desirae realized that she would have to watch what she said and pull her cards out of her hand at the right time.

"I'm off tonight," Desirae said. "I mean, you ain't gotta come over here if you don't want to. We can meet some place if you would rather do that. I mean, it's whatever. Hell, I can even come over and see you at your place." Desirae snickered.

Tron could hear the snicker and had to hold a groan back through the phone at the fact that his side chick now knew where he lived and where he made his money. Tron had a hard time dealing with all of that.

"Look, I don't know if I'm ready to talk yet," Tron came out and said. "I mean, that shit you and Shawna did, jumpin' on a nigga and shit, was pretty foul."

"Well, I mean," Desirae said. "What do you call what you did? Having one chick at home and another on the other side of town? Stringing her along and really making her think that you gon' love her and be with her."

"Desirae," Tron said. "I never said that shit to you. I may have said that I wasn't happy with my situation, but I didn't say I was gon' go be with you."

Desirae could already sense an argument coming out of the conversation, and she did not want it to go that way. "Look, Tron," she said in a stern voice. "I know what you think and what you saying. I know. That's why I was just calling to ask when we could get together and talk and really get a plan together. I mean, if you wanna talk on the phone about this, we can, but I just thought it might be better face to face."

"Aight," Tron said. "Whatever. What you doin' in 'bout an hour?"

"Shit," Desirae answered. "At home, chilling."

"Aight, I'll be through there in an hour."

Before Desirae could say anything in response, Tron had hung up. The next sixty minutes would make up the longest hour that she'd had in a while. Never in a million years did she think that she would be plotting to come up with a way to depend on a man like this. However, desperate times called for desperate measures. And she would rather depend on the father of her child than to go back to depending on her mother. Each and every time she thought about that scenario, it practically made her cringe.

Desirae looked around at her apartment, knowing that she did not want to give up her lifestyle for the time that she was pregnant. In fact, the more she thought about it, the more she liked the idea of a little child running around her apartment. After all, her place was certainly nicer than the area where she grew up, back before her mother and father were really making any money to have anything nice like what they had now.

When Tron came knocking at the door, Desirae took her sweet time to get up and answer it. Just as she unlocked it and pulled the door open, Tron was knocking for a second time.

"Hey," Desirae said, softly.

Without even speaking, Tron walked right into the apartment. "So, I'm here," he said as he began to slide out of his coat. "I'm here to talk and shit, so what's up."

"Well, hello to you too," Desirae said, rolling her eyes as she shut her apartment door and walked back over the couch.

Tron couldn't help himself and got a good look at the back of Desirae's body as she walked across the room. He knew that it would not be long before it looked different. Even if he hated her guts for trapping him by not taking her birth control, he could still admit that she had a killer body. However, her body could not make him trust her again. Deep down, he still wasn't even sure if the baby was his. For that reason, he was keeping his guard up when dealing with her.

"I went and told my mama today that I'm pregnant," Desirae told Tron. "That's where I was a little earlier, before I called you."

Tron sat on the other end of the couch, putting as much space between Desirae and himself as he possibly could.

"Oh yeah?" Tron asked, trying to figure out what that had to do with him. "So, how that go?"

Desirae shrugged. "If I wasn't pregnant right now," she said. "I'd be lighting a blunt up. It went alright, I guess. I can tell she disappointed in me and shit, but I mean, it's whatever. What are you gonna do, right?"

Tron nodded. "Yeah," he said. "I feel you on that."

"Yeah, so I'm thinking about using my mama's health insurance to go to the doctor and stuff," Desirae came out and said.

Tron nodded again. "Okay," he said. "I mean, that is one thing you could do."

"But I'mma need help with my apartment," Desirae said.

"What you mean you gon' need help with your apartment?" Tron asked, not liking where this conversation was already headed.

"Well, remember when me and your girl got into it and went to jail?" Desirae asked.

Tron nodded. The memory of coming out of the shower and finding Desirae and Shawna walking into his bedroom was still fresh on his mind. "Yeah, what about it?" he asked.

"Well, when I called up to the job to find out what is the status of my employment..." Desirae said then hesitated. "They basically told me there is no status."

50

"No status?" Tron asked. "Desirae, what the fuck is you tellin' me?"

"I got fired from my damn job, Tron," Desirae said, bluntly. "I'm pregnant and my ass got fired from my damn job because of your chick coming up there and starting some shit."

Tron shook his head and stood up, really feeling the weight of the world on his shoulders. He paced around the middle of the floor.

"So, now you done lost your job?" Tron asked. "That is what you tellin' me. I don't fuckin' believe this shit. I don't fuckin' believe this shit, I swear. First you stop taking your birth control and get pregnant and now you ain't got no job either."

Desirae looked up at Tron, who was clearly frustrated by the situation without even seeing the part that he played in making it even happen to begin with.

"I mean, damn," Desirae said. "When you make it sound like that, I mean…"

"Then what is it then, Desirae?" Tron asked. "I mean, so now you got me over here cause you need me to take care of your ass and shit while you pregnant and until you can find a job once the baby come? Is that what I'm hearing?"

"I mean, fuck," Desirae said. "I can take care of my damn self, but if I'mma be the mother of your child, I just thought that you would want to do the right thing and help me." She rolled her eyes. "After all, that is what you told me if I remember correctly."

"Well, if I remember correctly," Tron said. "You told me that you was on birth control. Next thing I know, you telling me that you pregnant and shit. Funny how we remember shit, ain't it?"

Just then, Desirae knew that she was all of two seconds away from getting loud with Tron. She decided, instead, that she would be the one to take the high road and not even go there. It just wasn't worth it, nor was it going to help her situation.

"Look, Tron," Desirae said. "That's in the past now. Look, I don't even know why I called you over here. I mean, I can just go ahead and move back in with my mama rather than beg some nigga to help take care of me while I'm carrying his child."

"No, no, no," Tron said, knowing that he needed to think logically about all of this. "I said that I was gon' help you, so I'm gon' help you. I mean, to keep it real with you, I got doubts."

Desirae leaned up on the couch, knowing that it was time to have a mature conversation. "Okay," she said, calmly. "What you mean you got doubts? I promise, I won't get mad or nothing. I just want to know. I think for this to work, the both of us both need to put everything out on the table and be honest."

Tron looked at Desirae, hearing the change in her tone. He sat back down.

"I mean I have doubts," Tron said. "I'mma keep it one hundred with you. I really wanna know if this baby is mine."

Desirae took a big gulp and looked away, not being able to help that she did indeed feel a little insulted that Tron was really running with the idea that she was pregnant by somebody else.

"Okay," Desirae said, nodding her head. "So you really think that I been out here fucking around with somebody else, Tron? Huh? Is that what you really think?"

"Look, that's not what I'm saying," Tron said. "I'm just saying that before I make a move at all, like any man, I want to be sure that this baby is mine. I mean, it wasn't like we was in no relationship or nothing like me and Shaw…"

Tron caught himself, knowing that it probably wouldn't be a good idea to bring Shawna up.

"You can go ahead and finish your sentence, Tron," Shawna said. "Ain't like I don't know who she is and ain't met her or nothing. I'm so over that situation, anyway. But okay… If that's what you want to do, then we can do that. We can figure out where to go and get a paternity test and once you see that you are the father, then maybe you will be able to put some of your fears to rest."

"Look," Tron said. "I ain't mean to make it sound like that. I just gotta be sure because we was just fucking around."

Desirae nodded. "Okay, okay," she said. "I feel you, I feel you. Like I said, we can find out. I'm telling you, though. I ain't fuck around with nobody else but you, even when you was only coming to see me every so often and we was doing the thing where I had to wait for you to call me. I swear, Tron. I wasn't on no other nigga dick."

Tron looked at Desirae then down at her body. "Yeah," he said, wanting to believe it. "Don't take it personal, but I thought you was on that pill and you see how that happened."

"Look, nigga, don't act like you wasn't the one fucking around on your chick," Desirae said. "And to make that shit worse, you gon' choose to try to get back with her even when you know that she don't make you happy. That is what I don't get about that shit. Maybe this is just a sign from God."

"A sign from God about what?" Tron asked, with a crazy look on his face. He could not for the life of himself figure out how getting his side chick pregnant was in any way a sign from God. "What you mean by sayin' some shit like that?"

"I mean," Desirae said. "The fact that we gon' have a family and stuff. I mean, keep it real with me like you used to." Just then, Desirae put her hand onto Tron's thigh for a second. "Tell me what it is that you just can't let go of with her that you don't see in me. I mean, I know the two of you got history and stuff." Desirae glanced down at her stomach while she knew that she had Tron's attention. "And I know you think that I did this on purpose, but I swear I didn't. That's why I was sayin' that it could be a sign from God…you had a past with her and now, maybe you can have a future with me."

Tron hyperventilated, hating the situation even more. There he sat, across from a woman who was supposedly having his child, and had all sorts of doubts and other thoughts running through his mind. Tron could tell by the look in her eyes that no matter what she said, she was really holding on to the possibility of the two of them getting together. To make it even worse, Tron hated that he was starting to accept that his life with Shawna was over. With each day, he was accepting that Shawna was probably not going to be coming back to him after everything that had happened.

"I mean, it's not you," Tron said, not really knowing why he'd said it. "And yeah, we do got a lot of history. I guess if I had met you a different way, then maybe I would see all of this a different way."

"Oh, I see," Desirae said, basically reading between the lines on Tron's words. "So, you only see me as a hoe and that is why you can't really see actually being with me for real?"

"Desirae," Tron said. "No, that is not what I'm saying. What I'm saying is that we started off as this side thing and now you talking about having a family and stuff. I mean, this shit is a lot to deal with."

Desirae hyperventilated then stood up. She walked over to her window and looked out at the snow-covered tops of nearby houses and the land around her apartment complex. She allowed a tear to fall down her cheek. It was followed by a sniffle.

"Imagine how I feel," Desirae said. "I was just a side line hoe, thinking that maybe all that stuff you was talking about your relationship with her would help you see that you really didn't wanna be with her. I keep my body tight; I keep my place straightened up for when you come over. I used to have a blunt waiting for you; even had something to drink, too. You never had to worry about no drama when you came over to my place, and I put it down on you just the way you like. She couldn't or wouldn't do any of that shit. I did. And now I'm the one carrying your baby." Another tear rolled down the side of her face. "I feel so alone already, Tron. I mean, you really just don't know how I am feeling. I am probably ten times as scared as you are about all of this. I'm pregnant by some nigga I wasn't even with. My mama done cast her judgment on me, as usual. I mean it's just so much. Then your chick comes up to my job and starts something with me and gets my ass fired."

Tron shook his head and stood up, knowing that he had better say something about it. "Yeah, well," he said. "I'm sorry about that part. I don't know what possessed her to come up to you job like that and do that to you. That shit ain't right, I don't care how you look at it."

"I mean," Desirae said, shaking her head. "It just happened at the wrong time for real, is all. I mean, I really needed that money. Now, I'mma be just another one of them single mothers who kid ain't got no daddy. This ain't what I thought my life was gon' be."

Tron slowly started to walk across the room. "I know, I know," he said. "But I'mma help you pay your rent and shit. I promise. You won't have to move back in with your mama. This nigga gon take care of you and shit."

"It ain't just all about that," Desirae said, now really getting into her feelings. "I'mma have to live with the fact that you would come over here and smash, but I guess I ain't the right kind of material that you would be with."

"That's not what I said," Tron said.

"Then what are you saying, Tron?" Desirae turned around and asked. "I mean, let's just keep it one hundred like you said. You sure ain't over here acting like you try'na with me. As usual, here I am the last to know. After that Saturday night at the club, I thought for sure that you was gon' be done with Shawna. Then, next thing I come to find out, you been meeting up and talking with her about getting back together. Have you talked to her since we left your place the other day?"

Tron shook his head and watched as Desirae turned back around and faced the window. "No," he answered. "I haven't. But, look, it's not that I can't see being with you."

"Then what is it?" Desirae asked.

Tron took a deep gulp. "I just don't know if we would work out."

"Why wouldn't we, Tron?" Desirae asked, really trying to understand all of this. The more she thought about it, the more she realized that she really did feel like there had been a connection between her and Tron when he would come and spend the night or just to kick it with her. There was definitely something there, and Tron was the first nigga she'd ever met who didn't see what he had in her. "I mean, you just don't see what you got here, do you Tron? It don't get no realer than me. It just don't."

Tron knew deep down that the reason he could not see himself being with Desirae was just because of how she was. In fact, the only reason he had ever walked up to her to get her number at the mall was because she had a body that simply couldn't be passed on and she was giving off the vibe that let him know that she was giving it up. The cherry on top was her deep throat skill. At the same time, he just did not see her as the wifey type. Right then, he looked across the room at her curvy body as she stood in front of the window, he knew that he needed to get smart about the situation and make it okay again. Without thinking, he walked over to her and stood closely behind her.

"Look, it's just a lot for me," Tron said in a very calm voice. "And it's not that I never had anything for you, but I just didn't think all of this would be happening so soon. I'mma be real with you. The last thing in the world I ever thought I would be dealing with now was having another baby."

Desirae rolled her eyes and turned around, now looking up and into Tron's eyes. "I know," she said. "I mean, I shoulda known that I was just a fuck to you. You didn't tell me where you live. I had to wait until you called me or there was little to no contact whatsoever. You was tellin' me that you was the owner of a restaurant. Here I am, playing Boo Boo the Fool, and have to find out from the news that you really own a strip club. I mean, how do I even know that your name is Tron? Well, I guess that might actually be true. The news said it, so maybe there is some truth to that much."

Tron wanted so badly to just let Desirae know that all she was ever meant to be was a hookup. However, he knew with how she was feeling at that moment that telling her something like that would probably push her even further over the edge. He pushed up against her backside and wrapped his arms around her waist.

"Would you calm down?" Tron said. "You know that I'm not gon just leave you hanging."

"Well, then, what is it, Tron?" Desirae asked. "Why can't you be with me? I just don't understand that. Explain that to me and everything will be good. Why can't you be with me? You liked coming over and chilling here, didn't you?"

"Yeah," Tron answered. "I mean, it was cool."

"And I never brought no bullshit and moody feelings to you like that Shawna did, did I?"
Desirae asked.

Tron shook his head, wishing that he had never told Desirae any personal details about his relationship with Shawna. If he had been thinking, like his boy Tyrese had told him, he would have truly kept their terms to just smashing and nothing else. Right here and now, Tron knew that he had made a mistake by spending the night with Desirae and doing anything that was beyond bending her over and digging deep into her insides.

"No," Tron said.

"I mean, I just don't understand," Desirae said. "I feel so unwanted right now, it is a shame."

Just then, full blown tears started to roll down Desirae's face. Even though she was turned away from Tron and toward the window, Tron would tell that she was really getting into her feeling and starting to cry. And if there was one thing that really got to him in the world, it was the sight of a woman crying. To only make matters worse, he was the cause of her tears. He realized, right then, that he had broken two hearts. Now, though, he just wasn't sure what he could do to make it right. He really didn't want to be with Desirae, but he knew that any chance he had with Shawna was well over and gone. He knew that the moment Shawna had found out that Desirae was pregnant by him, there was absolutely no way she would try to get back with him. It would take a miracle for something like that to happen.

Watching Desirae cry made Tron think about what would happen if he went ahead and did the grown-man thing. What if he tried to work it out with Desirae since she was having his baby? While the two of them were talking, she had brought up some good points. And she wasn't entirely lying, either. Desirae really did know how to make him feel welcome in a way that Shawna just didn't. Not to mention, Desirae had the body that he wished Shawna had just a fraction of.

"What?" Desirae asked, feeling Tron's body pressed against her body. "What is it now? Why you up on me if you don't want to be with me?"

Rather than answer, he leaned down and kissed Desirae's neck. He knew exactly what she needed to calm down, and he was starting to get into the mood to give it to her. If there was anything he had learned since he started to really get into smashing chicks in his teenage years, it was that sometimes all a woman needed was the love and affection of a man to make her feel better about everything. He was stressed to the limit and felt that there was no time like the present to pull that very card out for him to use.

"Stop, Tron," Desirae said, smiling. Just then, she realized how much she missed having Tron's body pressed against her body. And, as usual, he smelled so good. However, Desirae knew that she had to snap out of it. "Stop, Tron," she said in a more serious tone.

Tron was not listening to the words that were coming out of Desirae's mouth. Rather, he focused on her body and how her emotions were so high. A giggle slipped out of Desirae's mouth.

"Tron, for real," she said as he kissed her neck. "What you doin?"

Tron paused for a moment. "Helping you to calm down," he said, softly.

"Who the fuck said I need help calming down?" Desirae asked then smiled. Tron's kisses were so soft.

"Everything is going to be okay, aight?" Tron said, now talking sternly. "I told you that a nigga is gon step up and help to take care of you and that's what I'mma do."

"So, what does that mean about us?" Desirae asked. "I mean, what are we now?"

Tron hyperventilated. "Why we gotta be anything?" he asked, rhetorically. "Didn't we have some cool time back when we wasn't nothing for real? Why we gotta be anything? I ain't seein' nobody now. You ain't seein' nobody, or so you say."

"I ain't," Desirae said, smiling.

"Okay, then," Tron said. "So why we got to be anything. Why can't we just be?"

Desirae rolled her eyes and smiled. "So, what?" she said. "So you just think that you gon' be able to fuck your way out of this situation, Tron? I don't believe this shit."

"You know you want it," Tron said.

Desirae felt Tron's hand slide into her crotch and rub against her pussy.

"Stop acting like this," Tron said. "I mean, come on. We ain't gon get nowhere being mad at each other, are we?" He lowered his head and kissed the area above her chest. "Just calm down, why don't you? Damn."

Desirae walked over to the couch and sat down.

"Tron, I mean for real," Desirae said. "This is about more than just fucking." Deep down, though, Desirae could feel her own body getting hot. She hated that Tron was turning her on when she was supposed to be mad as hell at him. At the same time, though, she couldn't deny the fact that she liked that Shawna was out of the picture. She knew that men would say one thing and do another. At least with Shawna out of the way, and with her having his baby, that gave her a real chance. The more she thought about it, the more she liked the thought of not pressuring him. If he was smart, he would see what he had in her and not hesitate to wife her up, especially once the baby came.

"I know it is," Tron said as he walked over to the couch. "I know it. But remember how we both used to chill out after a long day. Well, this shit is like a long day. I'm fuckin' stressed."

Desirae smiled. Before she knew it, Tron was sliding her shoes off then tugging her pants off of her thick legs. She playfully kicked and resisted, but she knew deep down that she was giving in to Tron. That was what she had always done and with how high her emotions were running at that moment, she could use a little loving to calm down.

"Okay, this don't mean we gon' just forget everything," Desirae said, lying her head back into a couch cushion.

Tron simply said, "Yeah," and continued on with his mission.

Before Desirae knew it, Tron had slid her pants off and tossed them to the other side of the coffee table. Next, he pulled her panties down.

"Just chill out and relax," Tron said. He wanted nothing more than for her to calm down so that she could think logically about their situation.

Without hesitation, once Desirae's pussy was out in the open and her legs were splayed to the sides, Tron leaned forward. He pushed his head between her legs and put his tongue to work like he had never done before.

Desirae took a deep breath. "Shit, nigga," she said, feeling his tongue slam against her clit. "Fuck, fuck, fuck."

Desirae put her hand on top of Tron's head as he got good and comfortable between her legs. "Eat that pussy, nigga!" she said. "Shit, Tron. Fuck!"

Tron was relentless with his tongue, instantly feeling the way Desirae's tension and stress melted away. He kept going until he was eventually ready to dig deep into her. And just as he thought, Desirae did not resist one bit. There, on her couch, Tron pulled his pants down and dug deep into Desirae while she gripped his back. Tron smiled as Desirae's eyes were closed and she was practically in wonderland.

"Just enjoy that dick," Tron told her, talking very low. "Gimme that pussy and just enjoy the dick. Everything gon' be okay."

Chapter 6

"Man, I don't fuckin' believe you, nigga," Tyrese said.

Tyrese was leaning in the doorway of Tron's office toward the back of the club. Since the streets weren't all that bad, they decided to go ahead and have the club open that night. Even if the place wasn't going to be as packed as it normally might be, if certain dudes came in there, they would surely make some money off the bar. On top of that, they would get to kill two birds with one stone because Tron would finally be in the right frame of mind to really push talking with Tyrese about what they were going to do as far as making over the club.

"Nigga, don't make it out to be more than it really is," Tron said. "You know that was all she was needing to calm that ass down. She just wanted some of this dick. You know how bitches be."

"Naw, nigga," Tyrese said. "That's you. I don't know how them bitches be. Wanna know why, huh? Wanna know why? Cause I don't be gettin' they asses pregnant and shit. Man, you done really fucked up now."

"Why you say that, nigga?" Tron asked. "Huh? Why you keep saying that I done really fucked up now cause I done fucked her?"

"Tron, dude," Tyrese said, going into his fool convincing mode. "You know how females are, especially nowadays. So many of them think that if you fuck them, then y'all gon' be together. You know...doing that happily ever after shit. I warned you about how to handle that hoe."

"Man, watch it," Tron said. "She gon be the mother of my child in some months."

"Dude, I hate to tell you this," Tyrese said. "But you know I been your boy since way back. And I'mma just tell you straight up. Is you even sure that she is pregnant, let alone that the baby is yours?"

"What you mean?" Tron asked.

"What you mean what I mean?" Tyrese asked. "I mean just what I said. Do you even know if that chick is really pregnant or not. Man, you know how chicks be lying and doing just about anything to get a dude to stay with them. How do you know this ain't one of them kinda things? Nigga, you remember I told you about my uncle Charles. He only married that one chick because she told him that

60

she was pregnant with his child? Sound familiar? See what happen with that? Nine months come and go and the bitch don't even gain three ounces, let alone have a baby. He only wind up getting screwed and finding out that she was never even pregnant to begin with and just told him that so that he would change his mind and go back and be with her."

"Yeah, well," Tron said. "This ain't that, nigga."

Tyrese snickered. "Sure can't tell," he said. "The shit look like it to me, but what do I know."

"Exactly," Tron said. "Ain't you supposed to be fuckin' one of these girls or some shit up in here?"

Tyrese shook his head. "And ain't you supposed to be somewhere buying a stroller and diapers?" he shot back. "Dude, I'm just saying. I'm just lookin' out for my nigga. I'm tellin' you, man. You made the wrong choice by going over there and fuckin' her. If you think you done seen her act up, just wait till you see how she start acting now. You know how females are. I be try'na tell you."

"Yeah, yeah," Tron said. "And you just know so much about a woman's heart. How is Nalique?"

"Man, fuck Nalique," Tyrese said. "I'm on to better pussy and shit. Ain't got time to be even worrying about that shit no more."

After Tron dicked down Desirae real good, with the slow, long, and deep stroke that she loved so much, Desirae was practically ready for bed. However, this was Tron's time to slide on up out of her place. He left and headed to the club, telling her that he would hit her up so that he could get all of her bills and start helping her pay since she had lost her job.

"Man, I'm tellin' you," Tyrese said. "Before you start payin' that chicks' bills and stuff, I really, strongly suggest that you find out if she is even pregnant, and if the baby she carrying is even yours. You know how hoes is these days. These hoes ain't loyal."

Just then, Tyrese's attention was grabbed by a dancer walking by the office. Instantly, he recognized that it was the new girl – one he'd only met a couple weeks ago who had approached him about dancing at Honeys East. They really didn't need any more dancers, but since her body was right and she was thick in all of the right places, Tyrese couldn't pass up on her.

"Who that?" Tron asked.

"The new chick," Tyrese answered. "She gon' be taking Diamond's spot."

"You probably gon fuck her, too," Tron said.

"Nigga, I'm professional with my shit," Tyrese said. "But since you brought that up, then just maybe I do need to look into her qualifications a little bit more. We got a little while before the other girls start rollin' up in here."

Before Tron could say anything in response, his boy Tyrese was already headed down the hallway and toward the girl. Tron chuckled and shook his head. He was surprised with all the chicks that Tyrese smashed that he hadn't gotten one of them pregnant yet. Tron then thought about his own luck. *Shit, I done smashed half as many chicks as that nigga and now I got almost twice as many problems. I gotta figure out what I'mma do about Ebony's birthday so Andria won't start riding me about it while figuring out how to go about the Desirae situation.*

Tron dropped his pen onto the table and leaned back into his chair. He could not deny that with Shawna gone, his life really felt different. He wondered for a moment if fucking Desirae was a bad idea like Tyrese had said. On second thought, though, things were different now. He didn't have to worry about getting caught by Shawna because he knew that Shawna was definitely long gone since finding out that he had a baby on the way by Desirae.

"This shit is so fucked up," Tron said to himself, just thinking out loud. Never had he been in such a situation where things were as stressful as they were right then. In so many ways, he just wished that he had made a better effort to do right by Shawna. Now that the chance was out of the window, he really had to think about where his life was going.

***

"Well, girl," Shawna said to her sister. "I'm glad that it is working out for you."

Shawna truly was happy that Morgan had found a nice guy. Morgan was spending time with the guy – more and more as the weeks went on. She had even met his family. He was a young professional black man – no children, no baby mama drama. In so many ways, Shawna could see how her sister had really hit the jackpot.

Morgan smiled as she and her older sister chilled in her living room. "Yeah," she said, not being able to break away from smiling. "It's nice. Tomorrow he supposed to be picking me up and we gon go for lunch or something while he on his lunch break from work."

"Alright now," Shawna said, smiling.

While Shawna was indeed happy for her sister, the fact that Morgan was finally in a relationship and that relationship was going good only intensified how Shawna was feeling. Sure, she had a few more years until really getting close to thirty. However, she wondered what her chances would be of finding a good man before she got to be too old. It wasn't like the salon would be a great place to meet men. Sure, guys came in their every so often for this or that. However, if they were not the husband or boyfriend of one of the clients, they were probably gay. At the same time, Shawna really was not the type to go out to clubs and try to meet men there. As the days went on since she had last seen Tron, Shawna was learning more and more how a man can sell you a dream just to get what he wants but do you so dirty behind your back. She shook her head at that very thought.

"What's wrong, Shawna?" Morgan asked. "You look like you happy, but not really, girl. What's up?"

Shawna shrugged and shook her head. "Nothing," she said. "I mean, well, you know."

"You still thinking about that nigga?" Morgan asked, clearly surprised and not liking that her sister had such a hard time moving past the entire Tron thing. "Shawna, I was here the day you got home from jail and went over there. I don't even know why you still thinkin' bout that nigga. Don't get me wrong, Tron was cool. I mean, he was like my play brother-in-law and stuff. But that don't mean that I'mma just act like everything he did is okay."

"Yeah, Morgan," Shawna said. "I know, but it is just so hard."

"Shawna, do you hear yourself?" Morgan asked. "He made a fool out of you with some thot out on the south side. You go up to her job to talk to her and what do she do? She attack you like some animal. I mean, you cannot be serious. Plus, with all of that, you find out that she got a baby on the way by that nigga."

63

Shawna nodded, knowing that everything her younger sister was saying to her was true. "I know, I know," Shawna said. "Sometimes I just wonder if it was me."

"If it was you?" Morgan asked, not liking that her sister was getting in that phase of the breakup where she was wondering what she did wrong. "Okay, tell me this then, Shawna. What could you have possibly done wrong? I mean, really. Tell me. You was there for him when, in all honesty, he ain't have nobody else. Even back when you met his ass and he was deep in that street life with that nigga, Tyrese. You was still by his side, being his ride or die."

Shawna nodded.

"Then around the very same time you throw him a birthday party, you find out that he is fucking around with some other chick," Morgan said. "The part that kill me is how he tried to play it off like it wasn't happening…like I was exaggerating. He gon' tell you that he was making a U-turn. Girl, I saw him that day and he was not making no damn U-turn. That nigga looked like he was coming from somewhere. But, okay, so he had a little story for that. So, what is his story about getting the bitch pregnant? I mean, this shit is so typical. How is he gon' swear up and down that he love you and was even talking about marrying you after y'all move in together, then be fuckin' some thot and getting her pregnant? You shouldn't even be thinking about getting back with him."

"Morgan," Shawna said. "I ain't say that I was thinking about getting back with him. I mean, you've never had a long relationship, so…"

"Well, damn," Morgan said. "Just shit on Morgan today, why don't you?"

Shawna giggled and started shaking her head. "Morgan," she said. "Now you know that I didn't mean it like that. C'mon, girl. You know what I mean."

Morgan smiled. "Okay, okay," she said. "But still don't make what I'm saying not true, Shawna. So, what is it that you thinking about?"

Shawna was a little hesitant to explain to her little sister what was going on between her and Tron. Well, the fact of the matter was that there really wasn't much of anything going on. She had not seen Tron since she and the Desirae chick left the townhouse some days ago. At first, she was so mad that she could not even think of getting back with Tron. Now, however, as her days were getting lonelier, and she was not texting back and forth to Tron like she was used to doing, it all was really starting to settle in with her and what it would mean for her life.

"I guess my problem is," Shawna started to explain. "Is that me and him had so much history together. I feel like I can forgive cheating, but the baby thing? That is just too much for me to look past."

"I know," Morgan said, shaking her head. "That is exactly what I was thinking. I may have never had a long relationship, as you say, but if I was dating some nigga, and even living with him, and he got some side chick pregnant, I would be gone so fast he wouldn't even see me leave. Some shit you just don't put up with, especially when you know that you have better options out there, and there are better options."

Morgan could see the strain written all over Shawna's face, and she really did feel for her and what she was going through. She went from living in a nice townhouse that was laid out with nice furniture from department stores and stuff to staying with her younger sister. Morgan knew that Shawna was a strong woman, but at the same time she could be soft and pink. And she did not think that there was anything wrong with that. Morgan made it her mission, though, that no matter what happened, she was going to be there for her sister and that she was going to give her sister the best advice that she could think of.

"For real, girl," Morgan said. "Put that shit out of your mind once and for all. You know what we should do?"

"What?" Shawna said, hoping that Morgan was not coming up with another one of her ideas.

"I say this weekend, we go out somewhere," Morgan suggested. "You need to get used to letting some of these other niggas crawl after you and maybe you will start to feel better because you see that there are plenty of other dudes who would be just as happy to have you…dudes who at least, probably, wouldn't get some side chick pregnant. Have you even talked to Tron?"

Shawna shook her head. "No," she answered. "Not since me and what's her name was over at the house a few days ago."

"Good," Morgan said. "And if he call to talk or whatever, don't you even answer."

"It's just hard, Morgan," Shawna said. "I mean, to go from being with someone for three, almost four years to being just nothing, not even friends…it's hard. Plus, with how it all happened, it just make it even worse for me. I feel so betrayed."

"Then what could you possibly miss about all of that if you feel so betrayed from it?" Morgan asked.

"I mean," Shawna said, trying to find the words. "The love he gave me, girl. The things we had. The nice stuff. The place. The car. The trips out of town and stuff. I mean, I gotta face the truth: I never had that shit with no other nigga."

Morgan put her hand on Shawna's knee.

"Girl, it will be alright," Morgan told her older sister. "You will find another dude. You up in here acting like you forty or fifty years old or something. You still got time to find another dude and to find a dude who is gon' treat you right. I'm telling you, don't believe that myth about ain't no good black men. There are plenty of good black dudes out here if we black chicks just stop chasing behind them thugs."

Shawna knew a lot of what her younger sister was saying was true. She did start to look back at her life and realize how often she went after the guy that was no good while letting the good guy slide right under her radar. She started to look around at the black guys from high school that went off into the world and did something with themselves and married white women. At the same time, though, she could not deny that those very same guys were the guys who were getting absolutely no love from the black girls in school.

"You right," Shawna said. "You right. But I don't wanna go to no club trying to find some man. I don't think that shit work, at least it ain't never worked for me."

"Okay, that's alright," Morgan said. "We can go to like a spoken word kind of place or jazz club or somewhere a little more sophisticated as they say. You'll meet a different class of guy there."

Shawna nodded. "Yeah," she said, thinking of how going to those kinds of places might be fun. "I'd be down for that."

"Cool," Morgan said. "Better yet, what is your hair appointments looking like tomorrow night. I know this place that be packed, but in a good way with the good kind of people, on Friday nights. I went there once with one of my friends and really liked it. The drinks ain't real strong, but that could be a good thing too."

Shawna thought about her hair appointments. With all of the snow and how it kept coming in such large chunks like it had in the last couple of weeks, Shawna had appointments cancelling left and right while others were simply rearranging their times. She looked into her calendar on her phone.

"Yeah," she said. "Tomorrow night would be cool. I should be out of the shop by seven, no later than eight o'clock, I think."

"That works perfect," Morgan said. "Girl, I'm telling you though, we will get you a date by the time Valentine's Day gets here."

Shawna burst into laughter, happy that there was at least some way that she could see something humorous about her entire situation. "Girl, you betta stop with all that," Shawna said. "I don't need you to find me no damn date."

Morgan looked at her sister with this crazy look on her face. "Girl, Shawna," Morgan said. "You sittin' over here lookin' like this whole thing with Tron done really wrecked your life."

"You just don't understand, Morgan," Shawna said. "This is hard. And to think, I even met up with him and was talking about us getting back together before this whole baby thing came about."

"Whoa," Morgan said, hearing a new part to the story that she had not heard already. "You did what, Shawna? You ain't tell me that you met up with that nigga about getting back together. When did this happen?"

Shawna rolled her eyes and began to wish that she had kept that bit of the story to herself. She did not know what she was thinking by telling her sister because she already knew what she was going to say. Nonetheless, Shawna went ahead anyway and explained it all.

"I met up with Tron," Shawna said. "Downtown, in front of the Capital building like a night or two or so before I found out about his chick being pregnant. You should have seen the look on his face, like he really was sorry and was very worried about me and stuff."

"Girl," Morgan said. "I bet that is how he was looking. You know how niggas be actin.' That's probably why so many of them do so good in Hollywood. They know how to act the part and get you to really thinking that something is what it really isn't. At that point, you ain't know that he had a baby on the way, did you?"

Shawna shook her head. "No," she said. "I didn't know all that."

"Exactly," Morgan said. "Girl, listen to me now and listen to me good. I really think it is time that you let that shit go and find some other nigga while you still got time. You know too many chicks spend too much of their younger years chasing after the wrong nigga. I'mma help you out. We gon go to this place tomorrow night and we gon help you find a dude who is nice and professional and just not messy. Most importantly, no strip club owners."

"Girl, it ain't that serious," Shawna said.

Morgan nodded her head. "Oh, yes it is, Shawna," she said. "I didn't wanna say anything, but..."

"But what?" Shawna asked, wanting to know where her sister was going.

"I mean, do you really think that Tron was up at that club and not messing around with none of them girls?" Morgan asked. "I mean, you told me about what happened with Nalique and Tyrese."

"Morgan, girl," Shawna said. "But you know that Tyrese is different from Tron."

"Yeah, yeah, I know that," Morgan said. "But that still don't mean that Tron still ain't a man who is gonna do what a man is gonna do. What are the real chances that Tron was up in that building with all them hoes and not fucking at least one or two of them along the way?"

"I trusted Tron," Shawna said.

"Exactly," Morgan said. "And look how far that got you, Shawna. You trusted his ass and come to find out that he is out south with some other bitch who is probably doing any and everything to steal him away from you when you not even looking."

Shawna knew that her sister was right. She really did not want to admit it, but at the same time she knew that what was coming out of her mouth was right. She had indeed trusted Tron, and he used every bit of that trust to go out and do her dirty.

"Girl, you right," Shawna said, still a little unsure of herself. "We gon' go out tomorrow night and jus see what happen."

"Good," Morgan said. "Glad to hear it."

Just then, Shawna saw Morgan's eyes rise up to her hair. "Girl, what you lookin' at me like that for?" she asked.

"You do hair, girl," Morgan said. "So what you gon do about your head? I mean, you gotta give the men a little something to work with, to lure them in."

Shawna squinted her eyes at her sister. "Haha," she said, sarcastically. "You funny."

Chapter 7

Reese and Desirae were having a normal afternoon, just chilling in Desirae's apartment as usual. When Tron had left Desirae's apartment last night to go handle his business, Desirae admitted to herself that she was on cloud nine. The dick she had gotten from Tron was so good and strong that she woke up this morning still a little sore. As she would normally, she called her girl Reese to see what she was up to and if she could come through to hear a little bit about what was happening.

"So, you fucked him?" Reese asked. A confused look was written all over her face.

Desirae smiled and nodded. "Hmm, hmm," she answered.

"Girl, you stupid," Reese said. "I mean, is the dick just that damn good?"

Again, Desirae smiled and nodded. "Hmm, hmm," she said. "I mean, we talked about it all and he gon' support me with helping to take care of shit around here for when the baby come, especially since his chick is the one who came up to my job and got me fired."

"Yeah, that was some foul shit," Reese said. "But, I mean, so you still gon' try to be with him after all that."

"Girl, hell naw," Desirae said, instantly and without even thinking. "I mean, we gon' just be cool for the sake of the baby and see what happen. He ain't seein' nobody. I damn sure ain't gon be seein' nobody if I got a baby on the way. Ain't no nigga gon' try to be with me and I got a baby on the way."

"Yeah," Reese said. "I feel you on that. But I mean, you was just supposed to be talking to him. How the fuck you wind up gettin' some dick?"

"Girl, you know how it be," Desirae said. "He came over and we was talking. And you can clearly tell that he is really stressin' about this entire situation, girl."

"I guess," Reese said, really trying to make some sense out of this mess Desirae was in. "So, one minute you all mad and mighty and shit at him and you and his chick go over and jump on his ass. The next minute, you up in this apartment and he fucking the shit out of you?"

"Girl," Desirae said. "Don't make it sound like that. I mean, that's not exactly how it happen. I can tell that he still has feelings for me."

"Then why won't he just decide to get with you then if he still got feelings for you, Desirae?" Reese asked.

"Girl, you know how niggas be," Desirae said. "They be as emotional as females be. They just don't want to admit it."

"So, do you think that he is over there trying to get back with his chick and stuff?" Reese asked.

Desirae shook her head and rolled her eyes. "Um, no," she answered. "I definitely don't think that is going on. Girl, if you woulda seen the look on her face when we got out and went over to confront him once and for all about everything. She definitely did not look like she was going to be losing any sleep over that nigga anytime soon. I mean, c'mon. How stupid would a hoe have to be to get back with some nigga who was off getting something better and got that something better pregnant with his child? She probably over that shit."

At this point, Reese was quickly getting tired of talking about Tron. Her curiosity over the last few days had peaked at levels she had never felt before. More and more, Reese thought about how she had never seen her girl be so head over heels for some man when she could have her pick of any of them. To her it was just ridiculous. At the same time, though, it was making her think more and more about what Tron could be giving her that was so good that she was losing her mind. She wondered how much longer Tron would be attracted to Desirae. It was only going to be a matter of time before she started to show and had morning sickness all the time and gained weight. She wondered if Desirae was going to be able to keep Tron's attention once all of that set in. Or would she become some invisible chick with his child on the other side of town that he just sent money to?

"So, what did you mama say?" Reese asked.

Desirae sipped her Kool-Aid and rolled her eyes, grinning. "You know how my mama is," she said. "I knew that you was going to ask that question."

"Girl, you know how yo' mama be actin', Desirae," Reese said, smiling. "If I coulda been there when you told her, I woulda made myself available. You shoulda called me and I woulda come right on over to see this."

"Girl, shut up," Desirae said, swatting at Reese's shoulder. "I mean, she did her usual thing. She clearly was disappointed. She asked me if Tron was going to step in and help take care of his responsibilities. I told her that she didn't have to worry about that."

"And that's when you had Tron over here and you got some of that dick?" Reese asked.

"Damn, girl," Desirae said. "Is that all you think about? Is that all you hearing from me, is that I got some dick? Okay, yeah, he fucked me. But that still don't mean that I ain't tell it to him straight about what would need to happen. I told him I ain't got no job no more and that he was gon' have to help me pay my bills since ain't no job gon' be try'na hire a woman who is about to turn right around and be off work for maternity leave."

"Right, right," Reese said, snickering. "But, I mean, is your mama gon help you."

"Well," Desirae said, hesitantly. "I didn't tell my mama everything. I mean, I told her that I was pregnant. Duh. And she asked me who the father was, so I told her a little bit about Tron. Then, girl, you won't believe what she told me that I never had heard before."

"Girl, what?" Reese asked. "What she tell you?"

"She told me about this time when she was like eighteen or nineteen, she got an abortion," Desirae said.

Reese eyes bugged out of her face. She had known Desirae' mother for years and she always came across as the kind of woman who always did everything by the book and on the straight and narrow. To hear that she admitted to having an abortion was truly shocking. It was even more shocking to hear that she was pregnant at such a young age.

"Girl, you lying," Reese said. "Your mama had an abortion. Why, girl? Tell me, tell me."

"Well," Desirae said. "She basically got pregnant by some nigga, I forget what his name was, and decided to not keep the baby. The funny thing is though, she was telling me this because she had asked me if I wanted to keep the baby because of what it could do to my life and all, but that for her, she had wanted to keep the baby and so did the daddy."

"Oh," Reese said. "For real? So why did she go and get an abortion then?"

"Because," Desirae said. "My granddaddy wanted her to and she was just about to go off to college."

"So now she regret that shit?" Reese asked.

Desirae shrugged, thinking back to the look on her mother's face when she was sitting across from her last night. "I don't know," she said. "I don't know if I would say that she regrets it, but I could tell when I was talking to her that it is definitely something that she prolly think about from time to time."

"I see," Reese said. "That is a big deal, abortion, especially if you wanted to keep the baby. So, is she trying to hint around to you that maybe you should consider abortion or something?"

"Girl, I don't know," Desirae said.

"Are you still thinking about it?" Reese asked, deciding to just unload the question once and for all rather than to dance around it as if it was not a factor.

Desirae paused then shook her head. "Naw," she said, rubbing her stomach. "I want to keep my baby. At first, I really didn't know. But now I done talked to Tron and he seems like he might be finally coming around to us being together after I really talked to him about everything last night."

"Before he got some pussy," Reese interjected.

Desirae's eyes cut to her girl Reese. "Girl, would you calm down."

Reese snickered. "Okay, okay, I'll stop," she said, waving her hands side to side. "So, anyway, girl, I mean you done been saying that he was coming around. Then, the time comes and he just isn't around to the idea."

"Yeah, I know," Desirae said. "And you know what?"

"What?"

"I'm coo with that," Desirae said. "I mean, even if we don't wind up being together right away, you know it takes some niggas a little longer to grow up. Once he see that ain't shit out there better for him, he ain't gon have no choice but to be with the woman who already got his baby."

"Wait a minute," Reese said, thinking back to when Desirae had first started talking to this guy Tron. "Didn't you tell me that that nigga had a baby already when you met?"

Desirae nodded her head. "Yeah, girl," she answered. "He got a daughter or something, down in Louisville where the rest of his family is."

"I see," Reese said.

Desirae could pick up on the tone in Reese's voice and wanted to know what it was all about.

"So why you ask that, Reese?" Desirae asked. "Why you ask about his daughter?"

"Cause, I mean," Reese said. "I just wonder if you done thought about how much you know about the daughter. I mean, do he help take care of her or what?"

Desirae paused for a moment while she thought about it. The fact of the matter was that Tron talked about what was going on with his family and his chick. However, he rarely, if ever after the first time, brought up his daughter down in Louisville. The more she thought about it, the more she was coming to grips with the fact that there were so many things she just did not know about Tron. And realizing that was not sitting well with her.

Desirae shrugged. "Girl, I don't know," she said. "But he gon' help take care of this one."

Just then, it occurred to Reese that she needed to look at the time. When she did, she found that it was getting a little late in the evening and she was supposed to help her family with a couple of things.

"Girl, I gotta go," Reese said, standing up.

"Oh, that's right," Desirae said. "I forgot you said you gotta head over to your uncle's place or something."

Reese hyperventilated. "Yeah," she said. "Being the good family member and helping everybody get back on their feet. I can't lie, though. All this snow makes helping people twice as hard."

"I bet it do," Desirae said, watching her best friend slide into her coat over by the door. "But that's good. Reese, I mean, you are like the only person I really trust right now. I mean that. Thank you so much for coming through and talking to me about all of this. You just don't know how scared I am about all of this. I thought telling my mama was going to help a bit, and it did a little, but it really just made me even more scared. I just hope that Tron don't back out on me and stuff."

"Desirae," Reese said. "You know that whatever happen, I'mma be here for you. I promise."

Just then, the two of them hugged and Desirae saw Reese out the door.

The entire time it took Reese to walk down to the parking lot and get into her car, thoughts were racing through her mind. Deep down inside throughout Desirae's entire situation, she could not help the curiosity building inside of her. She wanted so bad to know what was it about Tron that was driving Desirae to go back and forth in her thinking. She had known her girl for years and never had she seen her act this way, so it was really starting to make her think.

Reese thought about her own love life. She had thought that she wanted to be in a relationship. However, as she was approaching her mid-twenties, she was giving more thought to maybe going back to school and getting an education. On that note, she was really starting to think about how she just wanted a hook up and to not have anything serious since she did not know where she was going with her life.

Reese warmed her car up and pulled out of the parking lot of Desirae's apartment complex. When she got out to the main road and started to head toward downtown, she could not help but think more and more about Tron. Even though she had only gotten a glimpse of him when she was hiding in the back room, everything about him was certainly on point. Not only did he drive a nice car, but he also walked with some swag and dressed nicely. To make things even better, at least to Reese, was the fact that he made his own money by owning his own business. At the same time, though, Reese knew that she could not blame a man like that for not wanting to be with her girl Desirae. Sure, Desirae was like a sister to her. However, even with her body that she loved so much, Reese knew that there were plenty of men who would see her and what she had going and just see her as a fuck or something to do in their spare time. This was evident with what was happening with Tron. And Reese felt so sorry for Desirae that she just could not see that.

A thought popped into Reese's head as she remembered what kind of car Tron had gotten into when he had left that day while she was in the back bedroom. Reese decided that instead of hopping on the highway and heading out east, like she normally would from the south side, she would go ahead and ride through downtown and ride by Honeys East, just to have a look. As she got closer and closer to the place, she started to get nervous. She had no plans for whatever she might accomplish by riding by the place, but her car just seemed to be headed that way.

When Reese rolled by Honeys East, after hitting a bit of traffic coming through downtown, she saw two cars parked out in the parking lot. One was an SUV while the other was a four-door. When she saw the same vehicle that she had seen that day at Desirae's, her lips formed into a smile. Right then and there, she decided that maybe tomorrow night, which was Friday night, she would get herself together and walk up into Honeys East. If nothing else, she wanted to see, and maybe meet, what exactly Desirae was all over town acting like a fool over. It was really starting to bug Reese, and curiosity was really getting the best of her. She just had to see.

***

Tron could not drown out the clapping noise that was coming from the other room at the back of the club. Not to his surprise, Tyrese was smashing one of the girls – which one, Tron did not know – when Tron got to the club.

"Nigga, hurry the fuck up!" Tron yelled. "You know the contractor is gonna be here any minute!"

"Nigga, fuck you," Tyrese yelled. Following that, he asked the girl if she liked the dick. She moaned loudly, telling him yes and telling him just how good it was.

Tron shook his head and snickered. "That nigga," he said. "All he do is fuck bitches. That's my boy Tyrese, though."

Just as Tron was turning back to his computer to look over emails, thankful that the last few nights at the club had been peaceful, probably because of the snow, his phone rang. It was Andria.

"Fuck," he said, to himself. "What the fuck she want?"

Tron picked his phone up, knowing that he had too much on his plate for any extra shit.

"Hello?" he said, sounding short.

"Well, hello to you too," Andria said. "Did I catch you at a bad time?"

Tron shook his head, thinking, *You always do.*

"Naw," he lied. "Wassup, Andria? I got an appointment in a minute to meet with a contractor, so what is it?"

"Well," Andria said, hesitantly. "Ebony is crying."

"Crying?" Tron asked. "About what? What the fuck she crying about?"

"Cause she really wanna spend some time with her daddy," Andria said. "Look, I know what you said about the weather and stuff, but can you please find a way to do something with her. C'mon, Tron."

"I told you this, already," Tron said.

Just then, Tyrese walked up to the door. He was buckling his belt buckle and getting himself back together, grinning from ear to ear. "Whew," he said. "That was some good pussy."

Out of reflex, Tron held the phone far away from his ear while Andria was talking. "Damn, nigga," he said quietly.

"Oh, my bad," Tyrese said. He then turned around and started talking to a thick little red-bone chick who was walking by the office door – the chick he'd just been smashing in the dressing room like there was no tomorrow.

Tron got back onto the phone with Andria, grunting about how she always managed to call at the worst possible times. He stopped her in her sentence. "Andria, Andria," he said. "I told you that right now with business and what is going on with Shawna that we wouldn't be able to do no trip of any kind for at least a few weeks. Tell her that she can wait until spring, you know, when it get a little warm out and we don't have to worry about all this snow and ice. You know how February be, especially up north."

"I know, I know," Andria said. "But why don't you call her yourself, Tron? She said she ain't talked to her daddy in like a couple weeks, I guess since whatever you fucked up with Shawna."

"Hold up," Tron said. "Who the fuck said I fucked anything up?"

"Oh, so you didn't?" Andria asked.

"I thought we agreed to not be up in each other's love lives, Andria," Tron said. "Ain't that what we said? I mean, you know I'mma come down, or at least try to, and see her for her birthday. I ain't never missed a birthday."

"Tron, fuck all that," Andria said, starting to sound impatient about the situation. "I'mma bring her up to you. I can drive in the snow. I'mma bring your little daughter right on up to you."

Chapter 8

Once the contractor left after talking to Tron and Tyrese about what it would cost to redo the outside of the club so it would look totally different from what people have seen on the news, Tron looked at his boy Tyrese.

"Man, this shit is just getting to be too much for me," Tron said.

"Why?" Tyrese asked. "Wassup?"

"Andria talking about bringing Ebony up to spend some time with me in the next week or two," Tron said, shaking his head. "Whenever she feel like it."

"Oh, yeah?" Tyrese asked, glad that he did not have those kinds of problems.

Tron shook his head as the two of them walked back inside of the building to get ready for a Thursday night. "Yeah," he said. "She trippin'."

"Man, sucks to be you," Tyrese said. "Glad I ain't gotta deal with that shit. You got baby-mama problems, wifey problems, side chick problems, and future baby-mama problems." Tyrese laughed.

"Nigga, fuck you," Tron said.

"I'm just saying," Tyrese said.

That night at the club was usual business for a Thursday night in early February. It stopped snowing for awhile, so some local dudes slipped away from their women for awhile to come watch some honeys dance on the poles. The place wasn't packed, but Tron was still happy at the end of the night. They turned a profit before they shut the doors. To make things even better, there was no drama or anything to cause a problem. It was a smooth night and he was so happy about that, considering what all he had going on between Desirae and Andria. For a second, as he and Tyrese were finishing up everything, the idea that Desirae and Andria knew one another popped into his mind. He shook it off, saying that all of this happening at one time was just a coincidence and that he would get through it like he did any other hard time in his life.

Tron and Tyrese pulled up at the townhouse around the same time and walked inside together. Tron still found it odd that his boy was staying with him, and he wondered how long it was going to last. Sure, he liked chillin' with his boy as he always did. However, being business partners and staying together, at times, could be a little too much. In so many ways, Tron was starting to feel older than Tyrese. There were times that Tron just wanted to chill out. Tyrese, on the other hand, was always about the turn up. If he could have some hoes over every night of the week, he would.

"Nigga, I need to smoke," Tron said as the two of them came into the house.

"Man, I know what you mean," Tyrese said. "I got a couple grams we can roll up and smoke, if you up to it."

"Hell yeah," Tron said.

The two of them did whatever they needed to do – get something to drink, use the bathroom, whatever – before meeting in the living room and sitting on the couch. Tyrese looked over at his boy Tron as he rolled the blunt.

"Man, what the fuck is up with you?" Tyrese asked. "You really lettin' all this shit get to you, ain't you?"

"Nigga, what you mean," Tron said. "I ain't got no choice. I got a fuckin' baby on the way by some bitch I was just supposed to be fuckin. And…"

"Nigga, I told you about that shit," Tyrese said. "And now you done went over there again and fucked her. Betta hope that her ass don't get pregnant with twins and it be one of them buy one get one free situations."

"Nigga, you stupid," Tron said.

Tyrese laughed.

"Naw, but for real, though," Tron said. "I mean, Desirae talkin' bout she gon' need help with the bills since she done lost her job and shit."

"Yeah, I remember you tellin' me that," Tyrese said. "That shit sound rough to me. You think she gon start a bunch of shit over it?"

"Man, I hope not," Tron said. "I'mma just give her some fuckin' money every month, once she tell me what her bills and stuff are and everything. But once that baby get here and she back to normal and stuff, she gon have to go out and get a damn job again. I ain't gon be that chick's meal ticket."

"Man, you know this is practically a woman's world now," Tyrese said. "You gon' have to be whatever the fuck she want you to be. If she want to go downtown and put you on child support, then she gon' do that and the courts are gon' give her whatever it is that she want and ain't shit that you gon' be able to do about it."

"Man, whatever," Tron said, not even wanting to hear what Tyrese was saying. "Hurry up and roll that shit up so we can smoke that shit. Man, my life fuckin' sucks right now."

Tyrese chuckled as he finished rolling the blunt. When he was done, he handed it to Tron and nodded.

"You first," Tyrese said. "And make sure you hit that shit good. I got it from what's-his-name, that nigga over on College. I don't know how good it is, but as long as it gets us high and shit, I really don't give a fuck."

"I feel you on that," Tron said. He lit the blunt and took a deep hit. "Man, this shit feel good."

"Good," Tyrese said. "Glad to hear it."

Tron and Tyrese talked to each other for some minutes as they passed the blunt back and forth on the couch.

"Man, you still thinking about Shawna, ain't you?" Tyrese asked.

"What the fuck made you say that?" Tron asked.

"Nigga, I know you," Tyrese said. "And I can tell when you really fucked up, cause you my boy and shit. You talkin' and shit, but not like you would normally be. That's why I can tell something is up, and I think that that something is more than just Desirae being pregnant."

"Yeah, man," Tron said. "I mean, the Desirae thing is so fucked up. And I swear she did that shit to trap me to trying to be with her cause that shit was all that she was ever talking about. But I can't even front with you, bruh. I have been thinking about Shawna."

"When you gon' let that go?" Tyrese asked. "Nigga, you know that she probably ain't coming back, especially if you got a baby on the way and shit. Don't take this shit the wrong way or anything, but she could already be talking to some other nigga or something."

"Man, don't say that," Tron said, shaking his head.

"Look, man," Tyrese said. "I'm just keeping it real with you, nigga. She could very well have found some other nigga to fuck with and now ain't even thinking about your ass."

"Nigga, fuck you," Tron said. "I saw that chick you was fuckin' earlier."

Tyrese smiled. "Yeah, nigga," he said. "That is Jamelah. She from Charleston or somewhere down there."

"West Virginia?" Tron asked, wanting to be sure. "The black chick?"

Tyrese shook his head. "Naw," he said. "South Carolina. And man oh man, she had some of that good ole southern pussy. That shit that is sloppy wet and be sloshing around when I was digging around in her guts."

Tron chuckled and shook his head. "Nigga, when the fuck you gon' stop fuckin around?"

"Nigga, I ain't chained down like your ass," Tyrese said. "I'mma keep fuckin' until I fuckin' get tired of fuckin."

"Nigga, you stupid," Tron said, shaking his head and laughing. Just then, Tron could feel his phone vibrating in his pocket. "Fuckkkkk," he groaned.

"What?" Tyrese asked. "What is it?"

"Somebody calling me and shit," Tron said as he was digging his phone out of his pocket. "With how my fuckin' life is goin' now, every time somebody call me, it be on some straight bullshit."

When Tron pulled his phone out of his pocket, he found that nobody was calling him but rather that it was text – a text from Desirae.

"Shit," Tron said. "It's Desirae. She textin' me."

"Oh shit," Tyrese said. "She got a leash on that ass."

"Nigga, fuck you," Tron said, as he opened the message.
Hey daddy.

"Man, she just sayin' hey," Tron said, telling Tyrese what the message from Desirae said.

"You know what that mean," Tyrese said. "You went over there and fucked her ass good and now she gon' think that you and her got somethin' going on."

Tron shook his head. "Naw, man," he said. "She don't think that. Man, I got this shit under control. I told your ass that I went over there and talked to her and we just gon' kick it like we been doin' since ain't neither one of us seeing nobody."

"Man, I'm try'na figure out when you gon find out and make sure that that baby she carrying is yours," Tyrese said, taking the blunt and smoking it. Smoke billowed out of his mouth. "You know how these hoes be. These hoes ain't loyal."

81

"Man, I told you," Tron said. "We gon' work all that out. I explained to her that I need to know, like any man would, since we ain't together, so I can just be sure. You know, for my own peace of mind."

Just then, Tron's cell phone vibrated again. It was Desirae again. This time, however, the text message was only questions marks – three in a row.

"Fuck this," Tron said, setting his phone down on the couch next to him. "I don't even feel like her shit right now. As far as she's concerned, with how late it is, her ass can just think that I'm sleep or something."

"Nigga, you know what she want," Tyrese said.

Tron looked at his boy. "Naw, tell me," he said, sarcastically. "Since you know so damn much about women and stuff, but got ran straight out the house by Nalique, why don't you tell me what it is that she want."

"Think about it, bruh," Tyrese said, going into his philosophical mode. "She know that you for real single and shit now, right?"

Tron nodded. "Yeah," he said.

"I mean, she know that you definitely, probably ain't gettin' back with Shawna any time soon," Tyrese said.

Tron thought about it for a second and knew that his boy was probably as right as could be. "Yeah, yeah," he said, hating how he had fucked up the really good thing that he had going with Shawna.

"Man, this is how a female's mind work," Tyrese said. "Now that she know all that, and where you work and live and everything in between, it would seem, she gon be hitting you up in the middle of the night and wanting you to come over. Or, shit…Maybe she gon' be try'na come over here now since she know where it is and that ain't no other female here with you."

"Man, she better not be doin' no more of her fuckin' pop-ups," Tron said, shaking his head. "That shit ain't even funny."

"Well, you better give her what the fuck she want," Tyrese said. "Or, I promise you, she is gon' make your life a livin' fuckin' hell. Just wait until she start getting into her feelings…them mood swings…from being pregnant and shit. Man, I remember when my sister's half-brother's baby-mama was pregnant. I kid you not, that bitch was damn near like a fuckin' dragon. Nobody, and I mean nobody, wanted to be around her ass."

"Yeah, I remember when Andria was pregnant," Tron said, thinking back four or five years – back before he knew Shawna. "That shit was fuckin' foul. I was so glad when she dropped that damn baby out of her."

Tron and Tyrese went on talking and smoking the blunt, enjoying how it felt to just chill out after a long day.

***

Desirae contemplated drinking a glass of wine. Sure, she knew that she was pregnant, but something was telling her that she had read somewhere that a little glass of wine was good for a pregnant woman. Furthermore, she felt like she had read that it was red wine in particular. She rubbed her stomach, glancing down at it and thinking again about how much it would change in the coming months.

"I betta not," she said to herself. Just then, Desirae smiled and sat the wine bottle back down onto her dining room table. "Let me see if this nigga done text me back yet or what."

Desirae walked back into her living room and around to her couch. She had messaged Tron maybe twenty minutes ago, knowing that it was around 2am and that he would probably be out of the club and home by now. She could not figure out why he was taking so long to respond to her since he didn't have a chick at home breathing down his neck anymore.

Desirae picked her phone up, unlocked it, and looked at her text messages. Still, there was no reply from Tron. She grinned and shook her head before throwing her cell phone back down into the couch. Deep in her feelings, she practically pouted before sitting back down onto her couch.

"This is some bullshit," Desirae said, out loud to herself. She hated the feeling of being ignored. In fact, she always did, and she really could not take being ignored by a nigga who should be lucky to have a chick as real as her in his corner even with everything that was going on in his life.

Frustrated, Desirae picked her phone up. She decided that she was going to send another message to Tron: *You still up?*

Desirae waited for a few minutes, with so many thoughts running through her mind as she sat in her apartment with herself and her thoughts.

"What the fuck?" she said, out loud. "Why the fuck ain't this nigga responding?"

Not being able to take the fact that Tron was not responding to her text messages, Desirae picked her phone up and called him. After several long agonizing rings, he answered.

"Hello," Tron said. His voice clearly let Desirae know that he did not want to be bothered.

"I know you see me textin' you," Desirae said, rolling her eyes as she glanced around her dimly lit apartment.

"No, I didn't," Tron said.

Desirae rolled her eyes, knowing that he was lying. If there was anything that she noticed when Tron came over to her place, it was that he constantly checked that phone. In fact, as long as Tron was up and awake, he was always checking his cell phone. Once, Desirae had even joked about it when he got into her bed and was looking through his messages. She had playfully called it blanket.

"Nigga, I know you did," Desirae snapped back. "So, anyway, what are you doin'?"

Just then, Tron's loud and deep groan came through the phone.

"Is there a problem or something, Tron?" Desirae asked, not liking that Tron was treating her like some pain in the ass.

"Naw," Tron answered. "I'm just tired is all. What you want? I'm tired."

"I can't just call you to see what you up to?" Desirae asked, smiling. "I mean, what is wrong with that?"

"Why would you do that?" Tron asked. "I came through and seen you already."

Desirae looked at her phone, shaking her head. "Nigga, what the hell is up with you," she said. "That ain't no way for a man to talk to the woman who is carrying his child. I mean, what the hell is all this attitude and shit about? I was just callin' to chat with you and stuff and you actin' like I called you while you was at work or something – at the club, I mean. I mean, I don't even hear no noise in the background so I know you not in that club. Not unless you layin' up with some other chick – some new chick, already."

84

"Naw," Tron said. "But I mean damn, why the hell you buggin' a nigga and shit?"

"Buggin' a nigga?" Desirae asked, feeling insulted. "What's wrong, Tron?" she asked, deciding to take the high road and be a real woman about the situation. "What is your deal right now? Earlier, you was all coo and shit with me… Now, you actin' funny."

"I ain't actin' funny," Tron said, sounding very authoritative. "I mean, damn Desirae. You be actin' like we together – like we a couple and stuff. Fuck, this shit is getting old."

Desirae could feel her emotions coming on. She was starting to lose her cool. She did not like the way Tron acted a certain way one minute then totally changed his tune the next. Furthermore, she clearly remembered when he was over to her place and him telling her that they were just going to be cool since neither one of them were seeing anyone. In Desirae's mind, this was her being cool. Just like she had been thinking earlier in the day, she knew that with Shawna out of the way, all she had to do was show Tron the love that he was not getting from her and then maybe he would see where he really needed to be. Like she had told him earlier, her being pregnant with his child at the same time he was ending an unhappy relationship could very well be a sign from God. To have him talking to her like this was just too much. She even started to get a headache.

"Oh, so this shit is getting old," Desirae said. "What the fuck is that supposed to mean, Tron? Huh? What the fuck is that supposed to mean? It sure wasn't old when you were over here and getting up in this pussy? Tell me, Tron, who you got over there? Huh? Just keep it real with me. Be a real nigga. I feel like you talkin' this way to show off or some shit because you was all up in this pussy earlier like the fuckin' world was going to end tomorrow or some shit."

Just then, Desirae heard Tron groan through the phone again. The more he groaned, the more annoyed Desirae became. She could definitely tell that he was annoyed by her calling. And she couldn't figure out why he would act that way all of the sudden.

"Tron, what the fuck is up with you, huh?" Desirae asked, again. "I mean, why you treatin' me like I'm nothing. I thought that we was supposed to be cool again. And now…now I call you just to see what you was up to and shit, and you actin' like I'm a fuckin' criminal and shit."

"Fuck," Tron said. "Girl, you already being a pain in the ass. I already seen your ass. Damn, can you just let a nigga breath and shit. I mean, really. I just got home from the club and everything. And I'm just sitting her chilling and here you go trying to force yourself into my face. If I didn't respond to your fuckin' text messages, what in the fuck made you think for one second that I wanted to talk to you? Huh? What made you think that?"

Desirae rolled her eyes and sniffled. She hated how much she got into her feelings, but she knew that she couldn't help it. A small tear had begun to roll down the side of her face. This all was starting to just be too much.

"Nigga, fuck you!" Desirae yelled into the phone. "Fuck you, nigga. You ain't shit."

On that note, Desirae ended the call. She tossed her phone across the room, into a dark corner where she could only hear it thump when it landed on the carpet.

"This is some fuckin' bullshit!" Desirae screamed. She jumped up off of the couch. For whatever reason, she did not know, she walked over and into her bathroom. After she switched on the light, she stood directly in front of the mirror. Every so often, when it felt necessary, she would have her mirror-mirror moments – moments where she had to keep it real with herself by looking at her own reflection.

"Girl, you are too good for this," Desirae said to herself. "Too fuckin' good for this. You pretty and smart and got a body that any woman would kill for."

With her fists balled, Desirae hit her fat thighs. This was all too much. She could practically feel her blood pressure rising; knowing that however far along she was with her pregnancy, it was not good for her or her body to be this stressed.

"Calm down, girl," Desirae said to herself. "Calm down."

On that note, she turned the bathroom light off and walked to the kitchen. She poured herself a glass of tea then sat back down onto her couch. At first, she picked up the remote thinking that she was going to watch a little television. After a few seconds of hitting the ON button and the television not coming on, she decided that maybe it was not meant to be. She decided that maybe she just needed to chill out and be with her thoughts rather than talking to Reese or having any background noise going.

Desirae sat there for several minutes, thinking about her situation. No matter how she tried to look at what was going on, she was screwed at least ten ways between there and Sunday. Here she was, pregnant by some man who clearly was not going to make up his mind. On top of that, she had lost her job because of his chick coming up there and starting some shit with her. Desirae shook her head, hating that she had let him come over just to talk – a talk that would wind up with her on her back on the couch and him digging deep inside of her. She was getting madder and madder. In all reality, Desirae was starting to feel like Tron was just using her for what she had. Furthermore, she felt like a fool for letting him because she knew, like any man probably would do, as soon as this baby came and her body would change, she was going to be either seeing him a lot less or he was going to be acting a lot funnier.

Desirae picked up her phone, seeing if Tron would at least have the decency to call back to make sure that she was okay. For all he knew, somebody could have come in and been holding her hostage or something. Not much to Desirae's surprise, there was no text message or missed called from Tron. He really treated her like she did not matter.

"Girl, fuck all this," Desirae said and stood up. "I'mma need that glass of wine right now."

Desirae walked into her dining room, poured herself a glass of wine and stood there, leaning against the wall that divided her kitchen from the dining room. She sipped the glass of wine, almost feeling evil deep down inside. She was getting to her breaking point; she was going to have to play this game a little differently. No matter what, even for the sake of her unborn baby, she was not going to have some nigga treating her like shit, let alone ignoring her and acting like she was a nuisance for simply calling when he had specifically said that the two of them were going to be cool.

"He wanna play games," Desirae said, shaking her head and taking another sip of the wine. "Okay, that's cool." She now nodded her head. "That is perfectly all right. I'mma make sure that he see me for what I really am. I am too good for this – too good to be letting this nigga do me like this. He come over here and fuck me all passionately and shit then do his damn best to ignore me like I'm just another one of these random, ugly ass bitches walking up and down the street."

Desirae made her way back to her couch, now smiling. In fact, she was on the very verge of bursting into laughter. She continued to sip her red wine, feeling confident that a little glass of red wine would not hurt a baby that could not be more than a month old. Plus, it was helping her to relax. Relaxing, she knew, had to be good for her and her baby. She just kept on sipping her wine as she sat there in her feelings – sat there in her thoughts. Right then and there, in the middle of the night in her dimly light apartment, she knew what she had to do. It had worked once before, there was no reason that she could not do it one more time. Whatever it took to get her point across, she was going to do just that and not feel the least bit bad about doing it. *It's a free country, right?* Desirae thought. She nodded and sipped her wine, deciding that she was going to have to pay Tron a little visit tomorrow night. Yes, indeed. Friday night would be the perfect night for Desirae to go rolling up in Honeys East to let Tron see what he was missing. She knew that he probably would be even more jealous by all of the men that she was sure would be staring her down.

Desirae looked at the time and realized one thing: she would rather move back in with her mother than depend on some man that obviously did not want anything to do with her. And that was perfectly all right with her. However, before she made her big move, she was going to make sure that she went out with a big bang. Right then, it was decided. Friday night, she would be up in Honeys East for a little chat with Mr. Tron.

Chapter 9

When the phone call ended, Tron tossed his phone to the side, not even caring where it landed. He just wanted to chill out and not let Desirae ruin his high. He looked over at Tyrese. With red eyes, he just chuckled – chuckled over and over again, as if what he had just seen was really that funny.

"Nigga, what the fuck you over there laughin' at?" Tron asked.

Tyrese shook his head. "Man, you, nigga," he answered. "You really got some bullshit going, don't you?"

"Nigga, fuck you," Tyrese said.

"Naw, nigga," Tron said. "Fuck you. That was Desirae."

"Oh, I know," Tyrese said, nodding his head. "She was calling that ass to make sure that ass was at home right where you supposed to be. Whoopah."

"Dude, I told you," Tron said. "We not a couple or anything."

"Tron," Tyrese said, just wanting to keep it real with his boy. "If y'all not a couple, then why the fuck she callin' you at two and three o'clock at night, in the morning or whatever? Why she doin' that shit? I don't even know why you entertaining that bullshit, man. If that was me, you wanna know what I woulda did?"

Tron shook his head. "No, not really," he said. "But go ahead, Sir Tyrese. Tell me anyway… The great womanizer."

"Exactly, nigga," Tyrese said. "You need to listen and learn some shit from your boy. I wouldn't have answered. Now you gon' really see her act up."

"Act up?" Tron asked, not understanding. "What the fuck you talkin' bout?"

"Dude, like I was tellin' you," Tyrese said. "She prolly over there feelin' real salty right about now cause you not try'na be up in her face. Just give it some time. It might be tomorrow, it might be next week. Shit, nigga, it might even be a month from now. But you gon' see what kinda shit happen when you ignore a bitch and she find out that you was ignoring her. Man, bruh. You know how females be actin' and shit. They emotional."

"Tyrese, man, just stop," Tron said, wanting to burst into laughter. "You really try'na act like you schoolin' me. But, dude, you ain't teaching me nothing that I don't already know. Been there, done that."

"Man, I'm tellin' you," Tyrese said. "I wouldn't have even answered the fuckin' phone if was you. How many times did she text you? Huh? How many times?"

Tron shrugged, not even giving it much thought and knowing that he was not going to go pull his phone out of the couch and look to see. "I don't know man," he answered. "Like two or three times or some shit like that."

"Man, then why the fuck did you answer?" Tyrese asked.

Tron took the blunt from Tyrese and finished it off before dropping it into an ashtray on the table next to the couch. He could not help but shrug at the entire situation.

"Dude, if you wouldn't have answered," Tyrese explained. "Then, she would have just thought that you was sleep or something. Nigga, by you answering, she knew that you was ignoring her." Tyrese shook his head. "Stupid nigga," he added then chuckled.

Tron stood up, grabbed his phone from between the couch cushions and began walking across the room, toward the staircase. "Nigga, fuck you," he said as he climbed the stairs.

Tyrese laughed out loud. "Naw, nigga," Tyrese said. "Fuck you. Better yet, wait till yo' new chick get nice and mad. She gon' really come and fuck you up."

"Yeah, yeah," Tron said. "Whatever."

"Whatever my ass," Tyrese said. "Just watch and see."

***

The next day, Tron could honestly say to himself that for the first time in some days he had actually woken up feeling good. In so many ways, he was looking forward to his day. Last night, he was a man about his business and let Desirae know that calling him and expecting him to be free to talk to her was not the way their relationship was going to be. It took every bit of him to not reminder her of what he said before – every bit of him to keep from saying that, deep down, he wasn't even sure that the baby she was carrying actually belonged to him. There were still so many doubts about that running through his mind. The very idea of her forcing herself on him before they even found out the results of any sort of paternity test was just too much.

The first thing he did was check his phone. In the back of his mind, he was sort of looking to see if Desirae had called or texted him back. She hadn't, lucky for him. However, Tron did see that he had gotten a text from Shawna, just about an hour or so before he woke up. Quickly, he pulled his phone off of the charger and into the bed with him as he opened the text. The message did not have any words. Rather, it was just a few periods in a row and nothing else.

"What the fuck?" Tron asked, out loud to himself, wondering what the hell three periods could mean.

For a few seconds, he lay there thinking. He wanted to make sure that whatever he said to Shawna was right on point. At the same time, he knew that he didn't want to do too much because he knew that she would probably still be in her feelings after finding out that his side chick was carrying his baby. With a little thought, he simply decided that he would text her wassup.

Within some minutes, his phone was vibrating with a response from Shawna. It read: *Nothing.*

Tron wondered what game Shawna was playing. And he sure was not going to bring this up to Tyrese. The last thing he needed was more advice from a dude who fucked any and every fat booty bitch that crossed his path.

Tron messaged Shawna: *You text me. I was just responding.*
Shawna: *Oh.*
Tron: *Yeah.*
Shawna: *I didn't mean to.*
Tron: *Oh.*
Shawna: *Sorry.*
Tron: *It's cool.*
A few seconds passed.
Shawna: *Yeah.*
Tron: *You alright?*
Shawna: *What you mean?*
Tron: *Nothing.*
Shawna: *I'm as good as I guess I'm going to be.*

Tron shook his head, really hating the situation that he had pulled Shawna into. Now more than ever, he really wished that he had kept those two worlds completely separate. Nonetheless, there was nothing he could do about it now. What was done was done and there was no going back.

Tron: *I'm sorry.*
Shawna: *Don't be.*
Tron: *But I am, baby.*
Shawna: *Don't call me that. And like I said, don't be.*
Tron: *I was just telling you, Shawna. I really am sorry.*
Shawna: *Sorry for what*
Shawna: *?*
Tron: *Everything.*

At this point, several seconds passed with Tron receiving no response. He figured that maybe Shawna was just texting him to see what he would say. He hoped that whatever he said to her would help, but there was no real way for him to know that. When he got tired of waiting for Shawna's reply text to come through, he simply set the phone down in the bed next to him.

"Fuck," he said, to himself. "I fucked up. I really fucked up."

Tron lay in bed for awhile, thinking that Shawna was going to reply to his text about being sorry about everything. She never did.

Chapter 10

"Girl, are you serious?" Morgan asked, looking at her sister like she could not believe what she had just heard.

"Why are you makin' such a big deal of out of it?" Shawna asked. "You act like it affects you or something."

It was Friday evening. Shawna had gone out earlier, in the morning, and did a few heads at the salon, before coming back to Morgan's place around 6 or 7 o'clock in the evening. While she was at the shop, she had one of the girls do her hair – nothing extravagant, just enough to make sure that she looked good while not tearing up the good hair that she knew she had.

"You talked to Tron earlier, when I was gone?" Morgan asked, shaking her head as the two of them got ready in the vanity mirrors in Morgan's bedroom.

"Girl, I told you," Shawna explained. "I didn't talk to him. He texted me this morning."

"But why did you text back?" Morgan asked. "Why would you even text that nigga back, Shawna? Girl, I don't fuckin' believe you."

"Damn, what is this?" Shawna asked. "Is this shit on Shawna day or something? Why the fuck are you making such a big deal out of this. So what I texted him back. What was I supposed to do? Just ignore him?"

"Uh, duh!" Morgan said, rolling her eyes as she put her jewelry on. "That is exactly what the fuck you was supposed to do, Shawna. I mean, I don't even get why you would respond to his cheating ass, Shawna. For all you know, that nigga coulda been layin' up in the bed next to his baby mama."

"I just wanted to see what he wanted," Shawna said.

"I knew this shit was coming," Morgan said, shaking her head. Morgan then turned away from the vanity and walked to her bathroom. She now talked from the bathroom, her voice bouncing off of the walls. "Girl, I don't believe you. I don't. I swear, I'm through."

"Oh, Morgan," Shawna said. "Stop doing the most. I'm not getting back with his ass or anything. Just because of everything that happened, don't mean that I have to be nasty and stuff to him. What if it was something important or something?"

Morgan stuck her head out of the door and looked at her sister through the vanity mirror. "And so what?" she said, shaking her head and rolling her eyes. "If it was something important, you shoulda told his ass to call the police or something. What did he say that was so important? Huh? Tell me."

Shawna shrugged, knowing that Morgan was not going to approve of the entire truth. That meant that she had to make sure whatever she told her sister was as positive as possible. "He was just texting me to say he was sorry," she said.

"Girl, are you serious?" Morgan said.

Shawna turned and looked at the bathroom. "What?" she said. "Just keep shitting on Shawna, why don't you?"

Morgan came walking out of the bathroom, making sure that her necklace was sitting in the crease of her chest just right. "Bye, Felicia," she said. "I mean, why would you even respond? He was cheating on you. No, I don't even call that cheating. Cheating is meeting somebody else and having a night of fucking or some shit like that. He didn't cheat. That nigga had a full-blown affair on you, and with some thot who work up at the fuckin mall. Then, to make everything even worse, you go up there to get some things straight, and you wind up in jail because she attacks you and you had to put them hands on her. I mean, I just don't know what the hell is going through your head. If you ask me…"

"Which I didn't," Shawna said.

"Girl, boo," Morgan said. "You ain't got to ask me. I'mma tell you what I think regardless of what you think cause you done obviously lost your mind. Anyway, then you find out the nigga was trying to cover up the fact that he got that hoe pregnant. Do you hear that, Shawna? He has a baby on the way by someone else. How can you even give one flying fuck about what he want to say to you? I swear – put it on everything I own and love – ain't no way that I would have even responded to his text message. If I did respond, I woulda told him that I hope him and his new bitch have a happy life together with themselves and the little bastard that they got on the way."

"Damn, Morgan," Shawna said. "You ain't got to be so evil. You going after the baby, too?"

"Shawna, calm down," Morgan said. "You always doin' the most. I'm just callin' it how I see it. I'm tired of holdin' my tongue.

94

You supposed to be my older sister and supposed to know better. Now I'm startin' to think that Mama must have dropped your ass on your head or somethin' cause I just don't know what be goin' through your head."

Shawna, deciding that she was tired of talking about what she was feeling and Tron, stood up. "I'm ready when you are," she said.

Shawna and Morgan stood across from one another, liking how they looked so much alike in the face in so many ways, but at the same time they looked so different. Shawna was wearing a really cute wrap dress that she found at a department store downtown. Her hair was lying down on her shoulders, looking lovely and black and thick. Morgan, on the other hand, was wearing tight jeans with a cute sweater that could almost work in any sort of situation. Her jewelry was what really set off her outfit, and she knew that she looked cute in it.

"Okay, okay," Morgan said. "We gon' go to this place and see if you can meet you a nice professional dude. No more thugs, Shawna."

Shawna rolled her eyes and said okay.

"No, I'm serious," Morgan said. "No more thugs, no more niggas who got babies. Only dude you need to be talkin' to that got a baby is one who at least been married and had his kids with his ex-wife. Screen these brothers, I kid you not. Screen 'em girl."

"Girl, calm down," Shawna said, shaking her head at how dramatic her younger sister could be. "I'm driving."

"You driving?" Morgan asked, confused as to how Shawna would just take it upon herself to decide that she was driving. "How you just gon decide to drive if this whole thing was my idea?"

Shawna looked back at her younger sister. "Girl, you know how you get when you get to meeting men and get a few drinks in you," she said. "Like I said, I will drive. Don't you worry your pretty little head."

On that note, Morgan rolled her eyes and decided that she would just drop the conversation. "Okay, okay," she said, waving her hand.

Shawna and Morgan slid into their coats out in Morgan's living room and each grabbed their keys.

"I can't fuckin' believe this," Morgan said. "I'm lettin' your ass drive me, at night in the snow. Lord Jesus, pray for us. Pray for us. Take the wheel."

Morgan followed Shawna outside to the parking lot. Little did Morgan know, however, that Shawna had other motivations for wanting to drive them to the club. Soon enough, however, she would see for herself. All the while Shawna was driving, she struggled to keep up with Morgan's conversation. Her mind was elsewhere, and she hated where it was. She hated that her soul was mad at Tron while her heart still loved him, even after all that he had done.

***

For the first time in awhile, Tron was having what he thought of as a really good night. It was a Friday night. The club was slowly but surely getting more packed with each hour. He mixed and mingled in the crowd from time to time, just to make his presence known while also taking the time to meet and talk with the different important people he recognized. The drinks flowed, as Tron could see with how busy the bar was and had been for quite some time. Sure, somebody was smoking weed. Tron could smell it in the air. However, he and Tyrese had decided a long time ago to not make a big deal out of anyone smoking weed in the crowd. Last thing they needed was to get into it with any niggas from nearby or big drug dealer names, all over someone smoking some weed. Tron just ignored it, acted as if it was not even there, as he walked around and talked to people here and there.

What was really good about tonight, however, was the fact that it was the first weekend in February. That meant the first of the month checks were out and people were spending them. If people were spending the first of the month checks already, then that meant that the retired guys were out at the club tonight and basically making it rain. Before the club opened its doors and got the drinks flowing, Tyrese gave the girls what he called a little pep talk in the dressing room. Basically, it boiled down to telling them to dance their asses off to make their money because tonight would be the night that a lot of the older guys had a little extra money to spend compared to what they might normally have to throw at dancers.

When Tron got a little tired of mixing and mingling in the crowd, he excused himself from a conversation he was having and headed to the back. A majority of the girls were out dancing on the stage or in the crowd, with just a few still in the dressing room because they had just got to work.

"Man, this shit is jumpin' up in here," Tyrese said, with dollar signs in his eyes.

Tron shook his head. "Nigga, would you calm down," he said. "What the fuck you doin' back here, anyway?"

Tyrese shrugged. "Just had to make a quick call and shit," he answered. "I'm headed out to the floor to talk a little bit and shit to people, see who all is out there. Anybody I should know of ahead of time?"

Tron shrugged. "Shit, not really," he said. "I mean, there's a couple niggas from over on Rural out there, then there's that one dude, the one I think is a pimp or some shit, sitting over in the VIP section with some hoes or something."

Tyrese's eyes lit up. "Oh, yeah? " he said.

"Nigga, don't go startin' no shit," Tron said. "Them his hoes, not yours. Fuck around out there if you want to and wind up gettin' your dick cut off or your ass come up missing or something."

Tyrese tapped Tron's shoulder. "Nigga, you know me," he said, smiling. "You know I don't ever start no shit. That's you with all the shit going."

Tron shook his head, hating how Tyrese found a way to bring up his new-found drama in any way and at any time that he could. "Nigga, fuck you," Tron said.

"Yeah, yeah," Tyrese said. "Whatever."

"Whatever my ass," Tron said. "Let's have a shit-free night, okay?"

Just as Tyrese was getting ready to walk through the door and out onto the floor, he looked back and nodded. "Yeah, nigga," he said. "I was just about to tell you that shit."

Tron kept on walking and went to sit and chill in his office for a second. Even though the night could not be going better, what he had going on was still sitting in the back of his mind. He knew that it would probably be some days, if not weeks and months, before he ever felt like his life was anywhere close to being back to normal. He had Andria demanding that he spend time with his daughter and planning on just dropping her off, which was coming at the worst possible time. Shawna had texted him, but said it was on an accident. However, Tron knew that she did that stuff on purpose.

It just made his think that maybe she was trying to forgive him for everything and just needed some time. He had decided earlier in the day, after Shawna never replied to his last text, that he would just give her a couple weeks, or maybe even a month, before he messaged her again.

Tron's head began to shake as the thought of Desirae popped into his mind. Something was telling him that he had made a big mistake by going over to her place and smashing her when they were supposed to be talking. He started to think that his boy Tyrese may have been on to something when he told him that doing something like that was only going to make her feelings stronger. It was ironic that she called him last night, deep in her feelings, because she felt she was being ignored. Tron had to take a deep breath just thinking about her, hoping to God that she did not cause more problems for him. The last thing he needed at the moment was any more problems.

***

Reese pulled up in the parking lot of Honeys East, noticing how packed the parking lot was. Part of her felt like what she was doing was wrong. At the same time, she had to be real with herself. It was obvious to her that Desirae was not the kind of chick that this Tron dude was after. She would not try to date him or anything like that, but since she had a little free time, and she hadn't been out in a little while, she just thought that she would visit the club a little bit and meet this Tron dude for herself. She could not get him out of her mind, just from when he had walked from Desirae's apartment building to his car. Everything about him was what she liked. While Desirae really was her girl and all, she knew that Desirae could only be the kind of chick that a man like this Tron dude – a business owner – would just want to fuck. She felt sorry for Desirae in many ways, mostly because she could not see what kind of chick she really was.

When Reese walked into the club, everything seemed a little new to her. She had been to a strip club two or three times before, but those visits felt different because she had been in a group of friends. At first, she had thought about asking the bartender guy if he could get Tron to come up front. Instead, she decided to take a smoother approach – play it cool, so to speak. She ordered a drink, sat at a little table, and waited to see if she would see Tron sifting through the crowd.

***

"Girl, are you fuckin' serious!" Morgan yelled, truly getting frustrated.

Morgan knew that she should have objected to letting Shawna drive the car. Instead of going the way she told, Shawna only went half the route she had said then turned and headed east on 10th Street.

"Shawna, no," Morgan said. "Why are you trying to drive past that club and see that nigga?"

Shawna shrugged. "I just want to drive by it and maybe say wassup," Shawna said, not totally sure why she was even doing it herself. In her mind, she was just taking a different route to the place Morgan was talking about. She didn't even know if she wanted to see Tron. Just as she had thought earlier in the day, her soul was crushed by Tron but for some reason, her heart still loved him.

Morgan hyperventilated as the car came close to the club.

"Girl, you a fool for this," Morgan said. "A damn fool."

Shawna snickered as she turned the car into the parking lot of Honeys East.

"And now we gon' go in and shit?" Morgan asked, totally not believing what was happening.

"You can just sit in the car, Morgan," Shawna said, as she pulled into a spot. "I'mma just step inside real quick so that Tron can see what he messed up on is all."

Morgan looked at her sister with side-eyes. "Hmm, hmm," she said. "Girl, you full of shit."

"Whatever," Shawna said.

"Don't have me caught up in no shit, Shawna," Morgan said.

Without even responding, Shawna got out of the car and walked up to the club door and inside.

***

Driving up from the south side, Desirae was content in knowing just how good she looked. In fact, she knew that she was going to turn heads the moment she walked in the door. Furthermore, she knew that she was going to turn heads when she gave Tron a piece of her mind. She just could not allow any man to treat her like she was nothing, the way that Tron had treated her.

99

Last night, all she wanted to do was to see what he was up to and he totally treated her like she was getting on his nerves or something.

When Desirae pulled up at the club, she was in luck. She found a parking spot not too far from the door. When she got out of her car, she looked at her reflection in the window of her car. There was a street light nearby that made her windows the perfect mirror. When she realized how perfect she looked in her red dress, even though she was a little cold in it, she headed right on inside. As soon as she stepped inside, she saw two people she definitely was not expecting to see: Tron's ex-chick Shawna and her own best friend, Reese. Immediately, Desirae's world got all the more confusing as she made eye contact with Shawna just inside the doorway, where the two of them had met the very first time just a couple of weeks ago. However, she really wasn't concerned with Shawna. Seeing her there let her know that Shawna was a stupid hoe and made her want to give Tron a piece of her mind even more. Shawna shook her head as well, knowing that she didn't have anything against this chick, Desirae, at this point. And she also knew that she was not going to jail over that nigga again.

***

Just as Tron was about to get up and head back out to the floor, he heard the door to the floor swing open. Tyrese came rushing back to his office.

"Nigga, come control your hoes," Tyrese said.

"What the fuck you talkin' bout?" Tron asked, feeling his heart jump.

"They both out there," Tyrese said. "And that Desirae is cussing some bitch out so bad. Dude, people is lookin' too. Come get yo' hoes."

Tron got up and followed Tyrese out to the floor. As soon as he stepped out of the hallway, he was looking at the backs of men's heads as they looked over toward the bar. Tron quickly pushed his way through the crowd of guys and over to the bar.

"Bitch, is you fuckin' serious?" Desirae yelled at her best friend. "You supposed to be my fuckin' best friend and shit and I come up here and find you try'na poach on my nigga and shit! How low can you fuckin' go, you ugly ass bitch? I don't fuckin' believe this shit."

"Your man?" Shawna interjected and looked at Tron. "Oh, so y'all done made it official now, huh."

Right away, Tron started to shake his head. He did not know what to say, and he didn't even know who the third chick was. Quickly, however, he could feel all of the eyes in the club on him. His stress level was through the roof, and he wanted nothing more than to have all of the women walk out of the club.

"Naw, Shawna, that is not what is happening," Tron said.

"Nigga, fuck you!" Desirae yelled. "I'm sick of you actin' like I ain't shit…like you ain't try'na do shit with me but fuck."

Just then, different men in the crowd made comments about how perfect Desirae's body was, nodding their head as they looked at her curves.

"Desirae, I don't even know why you try'na force it," Tron said. "I never told you I was gon' try to be with you."

"Nigga, I'm havin' your fuckin' baby," Desirae said then looked back at Reese. "And I come up here to give you a piece of my mind and I find my fuckin' best friend up here too, probably waiting with her old thirsty ass to try to get some of this too."

Shawna shook her head. "And to think, I really been thinking about you, Tron," she said. "About us. Low and behold, though, I come up here and she talkin' bout y'all gon' be together and shit."

"Shawna, baby, that ain't true!" Tron pleaded.

"Baby?" Desirae said, feeling insulted and yelling to the max at this point. "One minute you talkin' bout how you don't wanna be with her. Then the next, she is your baby. Nigga, just the other day, you was over there fuckin' this pussy and shit. I can't even fuckin' believe this." She looked back to Reese, who was standing there like a deer in headlights and shook her head, a tear rolling down the side of her face. "And bitch, I'mma beat your ass."

Just then, in the flash of a second, Desirae rushed forward and jumped on Reese. Immediately, men swarmed around as Desirae put her hands on her now-ex-best friend. "Bitch, I trusted you!" she yelled as she swung and pulled her hair. "I fuckin' trusted you and shit."

Tron told the bartender and the club bouncers to pull them apart. "Don't put your hands on me!" Desirae told them. "I'm giving this bitch just what her traitor ass deserve."

Tron turned to Shawna, who was just shaking her head. "I feel so stupid. This was such a bad idea, I can't even believe I thought about coming up here. I don't even know what I was doing coming up here. I'm done with you, Tron. I'm really through. Don't text me or shit. Go be with your baby mama and have a nice little family."

"Shawna," Tron said. By this time, though, it was too late. Shawna was already out the door. Tron turned his attention back to Desirae and this other chick – the two of them were starting to look pretty tore up from scrapping on the floor. At this point, the guards had them apart. Tears rolled down Reese's face as she talked about how sorry she was.

Desirae, with a face full of rage, looked back at Tron. "Nigga, I fuckin' hate you," she said. "I fuckin' hate you. I fuckin' hate that I even got pregnant by your ass and shit. I wonder who else you been fuckin.'"

As Tron was trying to think of something – anything – to say to get the entire situation to calm down, Desirae got free from the grips of the guard. In one quick swoop, she grabbed a fork from the bar countertop and lunged at Tron. Before Tron knew it, he felt the metal prongs of the fork going into his shoulder. The guards, of course, restrained Desirae right away. Reese took this as her chance to head out the door and disappear. Tron, on the other hand, gripped his shoulder as blood gushed out. Someone caught him as he began to fall to the floor. His eyes met with his side chick's, and he desperately wished that he had never fucked around with her to begin with. This was a side of a woman – a woman scorned – that he had never seen.

After:

The police were called and Desirae was arrested. This time, however, she spent some time in jail before a judge saw her. Tron was taken to the police department, and talked with authorities about whether or not he wanted to press charges. Since Desirae was pregnant with his child, he decided not to press charges. However, that didn't mean that the court system wouldn't do otherwise. Honeys East, yet again, was on the news, with the headline WOMAN STABS MAN WITH A FORK.

The judge went light on Desirae because she was pregnant. She caught a charge and had to spend thirty days in jail – the longest thirty days of her life. Her time in there was exactly what she needed to get herself together. She learned who she could trust and who she could not. Furthermore, Desirae learned that she would never be a side chick to some nigga again. It just was not worth the trouble. She would have to live with his baby for the rest of her life, reminding her of it all.